A Chase Like No Other

Arslay Joseph

Illustrated by Ray and Benedict Joseph

This is a work of fiction. Names, characters, businesses, places, events and incidents are either the products of the author's imagination or used in a fictitious manner. Any resemblance to actual persons, living or dead, or actual events is purely coincidental.

ISBN: 1511914858

ISBN-13: 978-1511914857

DEDICATION

To my family, who, with their unending love and support, made it possible for me to finish this book when I was just twelve years old.

ACKNOWLEDGMENTS

First off, many thanks to Mr. William F. Hanna, Mr. Bernard Mendillo, and, my middle school teacher, Mrs. Lauren Solomon, who all took time out of their busy schedules to not only give me valuable advice, but also to read and review my novel; to Ms. Betty Bogutt for all her unending support and motivation in making this book; to my two little brothers, Ray Joseph, for being by my side, reading each chapter as soon as I finished writing it, and to Benedict Joseph, who, with eager anticipation, constantly motivated me to continue writing my book until I finally finished it (they even worked together to paint the cover!); to my parents, Mom and Dad, for their constant love and support during the whole process, and, lastly but not least, to anybody else unnamed, who helped a confused, twelve year old write and later publish a 200 paged novel.

LEBRON

1

Lebron waited in the dark, lonely alley; he nervously shifted side to side, wondering whether he should really go through with it. What was he doing here? Lebron was no junkie, criminal, or anything of the sort. He was just a fourteen year old. He looked at his watch anxiously. Shouldn't they be here by now? It was fifteen minutes after the scheduled meeting and still no sign of life. What was taking so long?

Lebron sat down. He knew better than to get involved with these guys, but the arrangement had started up almost involuntarily. *Do you really want to take it this far?* This question still troubled Lebron, but now, he had no choice; there was no turning back.

A hooded figure arrived. Lebron's body unleashed one great tremble. Suddenly, he began having doubts. Maybe he should just go home and pretend this never happened. Soon, his shuddering subsided. The hooded figure approached him, eager to speak. Lebron greeted him uneasily, and gave his proposal.

* * *

[TWO YEARS LATER]

On the surface, Lebron's family seemed almost normal. Though his mom and dad divorced several years ago, nothing else seemed abnormal.

Lebron has three siblings. He has two younger siblings, named Sasha and James. They were fraternal twins, about six years old. He also has an older sister, Sierra, about eighteen years old. His dad, Charlie, took care of them. The twins were too solemn for their age and always seemed distressed. The eldest was emotionally unstable, especially when it came to matters of her family.

Lebron's mom was not involved in the family anymore. In fact, Lebron did not know how to contact her. She didn't even bother to visit or have anything to do with them anymore. She disappeared. And it seemed that his father didn't care, or was too nice to do anything about it. That was one of the things Lebron disliked about his father; he was too soft.

Lebron's mother was a normal mother, way-back-when. Lebron's mom used to love them, or so he thought; he had a hard time convincing himself that his mom ever loved the family these days.

The divorce was terrible, but the tension between Charlie and Lebron's mother had grown gradually. It started when Lebron's mother started to work more. Over time, she barely knew her children at all. She started to earn more money than Charlie, and when they both began to realize that, the arguments emerged. That was near the time the twins were conceived. Two years ago, they finally got a divorce. During the divorce, every night, Lebron, the twins, and Sierra would go to sleep with the sound of shouts and yells. Their parents' fiery arguments kept them awake.

At the time, Sasha and James were only 4 years old; they couldn't understand why mom was leaving. They cried, kicked, and threw the biggest tantrum they could, but they soon learned that crying did not solve anything They tried to be tough and move on, but they were still just kids.

After the divorce, they had a hard time adjusting to the radical changes. The twins became troublesome and caused problems at school. They began to isolate themselves from the other children. But Sierra seemed to take the divorce the hardest. Sierra went into a deep depression Charlie did all he could possibly do to help his daughter; he tried everything from medication to expensive therapy, yet to no avail.

Lebron's dad was also hit hard. Not only by emotional burden, but also the financial burden he had to carry. He tried his best to keep everyone in his family on the right track, but things took a turn for the worse when the divorce started. Charlie strived to give a better life to Lebron, and the others, but it seemed like nothing was good enough. He attempted to set a good example for them, but it was getting harder to be optimistic.

That was when Lebron adopted the job of helping his father keep his family together. Since then, things started to look better. The twins started to act their age. Sierra had become more optimistic. In the two years between the divorce and now, things had been progressing. Though they were still financially struggling, things were going great in the family. Lebron was happy to see how the family became so close. Things seemed perfect…until Miranda showed up.

Since Miranda had been dating his father, Lebron was always wary of her. When she started to go steady with his father, he knew that he disliked her greatly. She seemed so self-centered to him, and he never really approved of his father's lavish gifts and expensive dates for her. It was as if his father forgot how broke he really was and about his family in general. When they got married, Lebron's hate for her grew more intense as he got to know her. *She's definitely a gold-digger*, Lebron often thought.

Lebron hated the way she handled the kids when his father was gone. She frequently left them to do anything they pleased. She usually spent her time doing something other than watching the twins. Occupied or unoccupied, Lebron always had to supervise the kids.

To Lebron, the contrast between Miranda and Lebron's own mother was sharp. Frankly, Lebron's mother at least cared for her children, while Miranda barely noticed their existence. Maybe Lebron still had love for his mother, but nevertheless he felt that Miranda aimed to only take advantage of his father until there was nothing to take advantage of. Lebron also hated the way she put on the impression of a caring mother when his dad was around. Once Charlie left, she no longer has the motive to act as a mother figure.

Lebron has often told his father his concerns regarding Miranda, yet his dad dismissed it as 'normal child behavior'. Sierra and Lebron both suspected that there was something distrustful about Miranda, but his dad deems it to be nothing more than childlike suspicions. Lebron also loathed the way his father ignored the evidence and remained stubborn. It was impossible to get him to think about Miranda in that perspective, let alone her negative effect on the family and the family's financial state.

* * *

"Dad, I just do not trust Miranda. I have a bad feeling about her. I think you should be careful." Lebron said, bringing back the frequent argument once again.

"It's normal for you to feel this way. Kids feel this way all the time." His father Charlie said smoothly.

Lebron's frustration brewed. He hated the way his dad had no sense of importance when it came to this. He respected his father, or at least wanted to, but his oblivion towards the threat and his refusal to contemplate facts made it increasingly difficult to.

"No, it's not just a feeling, I know it. When you're gone, she does a horrible job at being a caregiver, but as soon as you arrive, she transforms into some sort of 'super' mom."

"Everyone has their own opinion on something; besides, some people may not be as good as babysitters as others. You cannot base a conclusion off that." said dad casually.

"No, dad. It's more than that. Dad, you've taken in a gold-digger! Do you think she would have married you if you hadn't emptied out your bank account for her? Dad, I know that she's only here for the benefits. Besides, she's just making our financial situation even worse." Lebron said with ferocity. "Dad, she is FAKE. Can't you see what's in front of you?"

"Calling her names will not help our situation. And I would appreciate it if you would respect me and my judgment. You're just jumping to conclusions as usual."

"Dad, stop being so stubborn. If you would stop and listen to me, maybe you could find it in you to-"

"Now, hold on right there. I'll have you remember that this is my house and whatever I say goes. You're impulsive."

"You know what? I was trying to help. I'm always trying to help, but it seems that you do not appreciate it. I made mistakes, but I do not jump to conclusions."

"How am I supposed to believe your ridiculous claims? Honestly, you're just bias towards your mother. Maybe if you could stop being so immature you could realize that she is not so different from your mom."

Lebron stormed out of the room before he could hear his father's response. *How could dad continue to persist on being the blind fool?* Lebron thought. There must be a way to make him see. Lebron never felt so unappreciated in his life. He had been trying to help his father for years, yet he was not given the credit he deserved.

As Lebron made his way through the hallway, steaming, he met his older sister, Sierra. She wore a solemn look on her face and made a gesture to comfort Lebron, placing her arm around him. Then, she made another gesture to lead him in her room. She needed to tell him something important.

*   *   *

After they entered her room, she sat down on her bed slowly. She told him to sit down. Lebron could sense the urgency in her voice.

"Lebron, remember when I told you that things were going to be all right, that I'll make sure that things are trouble-free for you guys?"

Lebron nodded, but Lebron felt as if Fate bestowed him with the responsibility to look over this family, or at least he thought they did so.

"Remember when mom divorced us and I had to take care of you guys and help dad until things got better?"

Lebron nodded once again.

"Even though I was old enough to care for you and Sasha and James, I cracked under the pressure and broke down. I will not fail again, and even though I've been supervising and leading you guys, I feel that I was not given the same amount of responsibility I had before. It's killing me inside, because I put more pressure on you guys during that period, and, no matter how hard I try, I can never make up for it. I want to help ease the pain and redeem myself."

Lebron wanted to comment, but the message she was hinting at was too unclear. Lebron knew what she was thinking; she was trying to delicately tell him something complicated. She herself was complicated, but Lebron felt that he possessed the ability to maybe somewhat understand her.

"Lebron, things are very hard, and you know that I would never do anything that would hurt you intentionally, and that all I want to do is to make you and the whole family happy. Always keep that in mind, no matter what happens, we, as in dad and I, want the best for the family."

Something was odd. "What are you hinting at?"

"I'm… going to run away –because right now I sense that things are going to go wrong. I know Miranda's game. Miranda is going to do what mom did. And besides, I'll be just a burden by then. I'm going to live on my own. "

"What about school? You'll ruin your future."

"I'm not dropping out of high school. I'm still going to college. I'll just take an extra shift at work and rent a cheap apartment until I go to college."

"That is not going to cover the bills of your apartment and pay your college money!" Lebron said loudly.

She put her index finger in front of her mouth to say "quiet".

She looked around cautiously, and then said, "I'll find a way. Besides, I still have my savings account for college. I could just save money from now on in a different account. Just trust me; I got it all figured out."

Lebron stood there, bewildered at what he was hearing. He could not believe what he was hearing. Sierra was trying to take radical measures to ease this burden she'd allegedly placed on them, yet her plan was not clever at all, and Lebron was shocked about her confidence and certitude in her foolish plan; he never knew she had so much naïveté in her to believe that things would smooth over if she took these measures.

The plan was too ambitious. Sierra has always tried to help the family, and Lebron understands that it pains her to see the family in so much pain, but there was a certain border between *Helpful* and *Irrational* that she was crossing.

Lebron turned away from Sierra, still pouting, and said, "Does it have to be this way? This plan is too ambitious, and it will not do any good to anyone."

"Come on Lebron. It's simple, really. I'm just starting my life as an independent individual instead of mooching off dad any longer." Sierra said.

"Why do you have to do this? We can still stay together. It's a dangerous world out there. There's so many things that can happen, and your underestimating all the challenges you'll face, and-" Lebron paused for a moment, trying to refrain from yelling, mostly crying however. "I don't want to lose you."

Sierra placed her arm on Lebron's shoulder, and said gently, "I have to do this. I'm 18, a legal adult. I don't want to make dad's life harder."

"Why are you telling me this?" Lebron replied quickly with a hint of spite.

"So you can explain to everyone why I did this."

"Don't do this." He said firmly.

She looked at him strait in his eyes. His attempt to refrain from crying was deteriorating swiftly, as he was starting to tear up, but he used the rest of his will to control himself. She then looked away.

Afterwards, she reluctantly said, "There is a possibility I will not go, but when things go wrong, we're going to have to do something."

She was deep in thought.

Lebron trusted Sierra's judgment; she was his elder sibling. She was an overall decent person and a good role model. She had a major part in shaping his personality, mostly Lebron's code of ethics. She helped Lebron understand the complex issue of justice and why it matters. She also passed down a great love and concern for family to Lebron, which ended up becoming a crucial and dominate element in his personality. Yet Lebron could never find himself to comprehend her train of thought.

Lebron walked away, dumbfounded and surprised. He could not believe what she was planning to do. He did not believe it. What happened to his wise, clever, street-smart Sierra? Things changed after the divorce, and since then, Lebron did not know who Sierra exactly was. Some characteristics remained, but she fluctuated too frequently after the divorce, and many of the characteristics she had one day would later be altered, replaced or discarded. In a sense, she was a different person than she used to be, but in another sense, she was exactly the same.

Nevertheless, Sierra was taking rash measures on a basis that might be false in itself. Lebron knew that his suspicion of Miranda was justified and supported, but he could not help but wonder… maybe his dad was right. Maybe Lebron was just jumping to conclusions as his father rationalized. Maybe she might be a nice, misunderstood person; that's a possibility… right?

Katrina

1

Behind every famous person is a good mother, or at least that's what they say. Katrina looked towards her daughter, storming off. *And what of the daughter of a famous person?* Katrina sighed. These things were out of her control, but she never understood why her daughter rejected her.

Maybe rebellion is in Garcia's blood, a voice whispered to Katrina. *You know your past.*

Katrina scoffed. *What's in the past was in the past. I raised Garcia differently.*

Yet the persistent voice insisted. *You cannot flee the past, no matter how hard you try.*

Katrina looked at her watch. It was about time for her to go to work. She packed her suitcase swiftly.

She hesitated before she walked out the door.

"Goodbye!"

All Katrina got back was silence.

Sighing, she left the house and went in her car before zooming away: she had a campaign speech to give.

Katrina thought about her daughter some more. She understood that being the daughter of any famous person was difficult, especially one so locally admired as her; she was the most the beloved mayor in the history of Shire Rock. Katrina shrugged off the idea once more and reminisced about her rise to fame eight years ago.

She was the greatest thing that ever happened to this small town. Politicians praised her for her work and even critics couldn't deny her success. The once turbulent city of Shire Rock adored her for ending the era of despair. Everybody knew that the name Katrina Hernandez was the name of a hero.

People considered the other candidate to be fake; he had little motivation and the only things he offered were promises. Those candidates were locally called "empty seats" because of their empty promises. Shire Rock couldn't handle another one.

When Katrina was running for mayor, she was interviewed by various different people and networks, most illustriously by a very famous talk show host. The show's theme was about accomplished minority females and the plight of a woman in a man's world. Katrina was one of the invited guests that they were going to interview.

The show consisted of three, but one enthusiastic Hispanic host, named Cheyenne, was the one interviewing her. First, they spoke about all of Katrina's accomplishments so far. Even though she wasn't mayor yet, Katrina was already a very influential person. Everything was going fine during the talk show, until one comment was made.

"Well, you're just a Perfect Patty aren't you?"

With this casual remark, her reputation was created. One of Katrina's supporters stood up in the crowd and shouted, "You bet she is!"

With that comment, the crowd agitated with signs of agreement. That was probably the turning point in her career from a small politician to a local legend.

At first, Katrina tried to be modest and end all of the commotion surrounding her. However, the remark sparked something big. At one of her campaign speeches, people started chanting "Perfect Patty". It became a movement, a crusade, a revolution against the typical 'empty seats' and a new beginning for the crime-infested city.

People thought that her principles, ideals, and political goals were somehow "perfect" for the plagued city. At debates, the audience stirred, and the seemingly civilized spectators began to hoot and holler "Perfect Patty" at the top of their lungs, walloping their hands against each other savagely.

At that time, Shire Rock, an already declining city, was further cursed with its sudden emergence of criminal activity. To outsiders, it was already gaining a bad reputation. In fact, it was rumored that a person could be robbed, raped, and killed by different people on the same day in Shire Rock.

Soon, her campaign managers took advantage of this gold mine; propaganda posters praised Perfect Patty piously, and people paraded across the city for the noble cause of electing Katrina Hernandez. Even the criminals cooperated; gangs filled with Katrina enthusiasts intimidated potential voters to vote for her. Various plots were created to assassinate the empty seat, but no one bothered to go through with the arrangements; everyone knew that she was a shoe-in for mayor.

As mayor, Katrina accomplished all that she promised, and the town worshipped her. Even though it has been about eight years since then, the name stuck and the accomplishments Katrina performed in office only confirmed the point that she was Perfect Patty.

Unfortunately, amidst all this praise, she lost control of her domestic life, and her daughter Garcia started to rebel against her. Katrina realized that her thoughts were going in a loop and decided to change the subject.

Katrina arrived at her destination and gave another campaign speech. People waved their Perfect Patty flags throughout the speech. At the end, the audience applauded and the people chanted Perfect Patty as they always had. Katrina smiled. These were her people who supported her and loved her. At that moment, Katrina didn't care about Garcia; she cared about her fans.

Jack

1

I was taking a hard look at myself. I was ashamed at what I saw. All I saw was a wondering soul unable to stay in one place because he wasn't wanted anywhere where he went. I was heading to Shire Rock, my native soil, as far as I knew, my parents lived. I wondered how my parents would have reacted if they saw me then. What would they see? A failure? A empty human being? A lonely spirit drifting between reality and the underworld in search of a reason to exist?

That night, I found a pillow and several bundles of large cotton balls; nearby lay a sewing kit and a patch of soft, safe looking grass. I decided to sew a bed out of the materials available. The pillow was already supplied, even though it looked worn out and contaminated. I set to work. I don't know why but I always had been a quick learner. After a few moments of trial and error, I became a natural tailor. In less than half an hour, I had woven my own bed. I spotted a hidden area under the highway that was invisible to almost anyone. It was a dark and noisy place to rest, but at least it wasn't filthy. I decided to sleep there for the night. What a disgrace, I told myself. But I had to do what I had to do to survive, even if it meant eating with the pigs.

That night, I suffered a nightmare. I was used to having nightmares, but this one was the first of many that really got to me.

I was walking in an isolated neighborhood and I approached a mansion. Not an ordinary mansion, but one so extravagant that you would wonder if the owner had to sell a soul to own such a house. When I knocked on the door, the doorbell sounded a magnificent tune.

The door opened slowly, almost angelically, and as I peered into the house I think I saw heaven. At least in a material sense. Suddenly, a man stood in the way, blocking my view. He asked me to identify myself in a bitter voice. I realized that he was just a maid.

After telling him who I was, the butler begrudgingly welcomed me in, and behind the servant arrived a rich family: a mom dressed in gold, a father in a jewel encrusted suit and a fancier version of me. A Jack 2.0. He had golden pupils and even though he was my twin, he had a cleaner, more handsome look than I did. He had an expression on his face that frightened me; his pupil glared at me as if he wanted me to fall.

As I entered, my father gave me a look of pure disgust. After spending some time glaring at me, he asked, "Jack, is that you?"

"Yes, dad, I've come back to you after years of searching."

He clearly wasn't moved by my return. He remained in silence for what felt like years.

"Dad, I'm home."

He looked at me disgustedly.

"Uh, What's that smell? You people are not sanitary."

After turning away in revulsion, he added, "Look at what a failure you turned out to be."

That comment stung harder than any pain I had ever felt before; this, coming from a father who abandoned me at such a young age.

"Dad, I came all this way so you could take me in, like old times."

He laughed, horribly.

"Can't you take a point?! Your mother and I knew you were destined to be a failure. Look at yourself! We didn't want to live with the shame that you would bring along to us. So we threw you away."

Tears jerked in my eyes. I tried to wipe them away violently. I was trembling, and my voice rose to an irritating whine. I looked a child throwing a tantrum. I was seven again.

"But I came all this way, suffering a lot along the way. I went through hell because of you. I looked for the slim chance that you might still love Me."

This time, my mom answered.

"Ha! You better get used to it. Failures like you will always have to suffer. They bring misery to themselves and the people around them. Have you ever noticed that as you suffered through childhood, the other children enjoyed theirs, yet they still will have a future, unlike you?"

I backed up against the door in absolute agony. My forehead was dizzy. My eyes were scorched. My throat ached; I almost choked on my despair.

My clone went up in my face and said, "You will never belong. You're a defect version of me. And you know what happens to defects? They get thrown away. But sometimes, they just should not exist. Sometimes, it's best to erase the undesirables from the big picture so they do not spoil it. I think you know what I'm hinting at. I'll just spell it out for you."

I covered my ears. I refused to hear what he had to say next. Even though I muffled out the sound, I still heard what he said. Deep inside, I knew...

A sudden flash occurred; all I could hear was a loud bang.

I was finally out of the picture.

I woke with a start. It was noon already and I was covered in litter. I stood up to see guys around my age surrounding me. They were littering on me, a whole horde of them. They hurled trash at me for enjoyment. They came one by one to partake in what they saw was some sort of game. Their cruel laughter invaded my eardrums. These laughs were evil.

I let them do it for a while. I didn't want to cause trouble, so I just laid there in the filth for a while. I knew that doing so was pathetic, but I didn't want to move. After a while, the horde got larger and larger and they got more and more trash. As the number of teens and trash increased, in the same way the things that they launched at me were getting more rancid, disgusting, and sickening. They started out with plastic bottles to unfinished foods and drinks to rotten mold, muck, and slime. I started to walk away to be the bigger man, but they followed me. Their insults became clearer than ever before.

"Look at it, trash man!"

"Look at this loser."

"Hobo."

"Moron."

"Bastard."

Then, one of them, looking a lot shorter and younger from the rest shouted, "The trash belongs with trash, after all."

It got worse one after the other. The situation became increasingly dangerous, so I had to run. They started throwing rocks at me then. By that time, I started to sprint. They wanted to stone me to death as a joke. I ran far but they caught up to me eventually, and soon I was cornered.

Soon, I started to bleed fluidly. That only made them laugh louder. I started to get angry, very angry; the type of fury that causes you to go into a state of rage. This was the first time I got that mad. Actually, this was the first time I got mad for as long as I could remember. I was prone to sadness, not anger. I started to throw sticks and stones back.

At first, I hesitated, but their insults gave me momentum. Soon, I was throwing rocks like gun shoot bullets; I aimed to kill. Yet in my blind wrath, I was struck in the back with what felt like a bullet. Apparently, one of the younger kids pegged me in the back with glass while I wasn't looking. The other kids were congratulating him.

As I collapsed in pain, I took another look at the person who threw the rock at me. Suddenly, his face transfigured into the face of the clone in my nightmare. It mouthed the word it said before in my dream. Its golden pupils mocked me as I fell.

After I stood up, I picked up the heaviest, most jagged rock I could find and hurtled it at the clone. As the rock hit the person's head, the kid's face transfigured back into the young face it was before.

I guess I did not know my own strength. The rock hit the kid in the middle of the head and sent him to the ground, unconscious. And as the blood gushed from the kid's forehead, it was obvious he was not even fourteen yet. It looked as if I fractured his skull. And as the others screamed and ran away leaving the kid with his big brother, I ran too. I sprinted and left the two alone. As I ran, the word my clone said popped up in my head. This time, it was much too clear to avoid.

Suicide.

Garcia

1

The door knocked loudly and aggressively. Garcia, irritated by the harsh sound of the person's raps, opened the door. A stranger stood on their porch; he was an adult, but had a youthful handsomeness to him, despite looking around her mother's age. He was light caramel and had brown eyes. He had dark hair, braided. Garcia knew he was Hispanic; she knew the look of her people. He wore all black as if to conceal himself.

"Is Katrina here?" he asked mysteriously.

Garcia scowled. He must be just another admirer. "No, she is not. Come back later."

It was hard to have a mother whose very existence was a sick propaganda machine. Her lofty attitude, her contempt for Garcia, and her indifference to Garcia in general was nauseating. To have her failures compared to her mother's accomplishments on a daily basis was demeaning. Sometimes, she felt inferior just by being in the presence of her mother. Garcia couldn't completely blame her mother for the arrogant 'Perfect Patty' persona: the public, media, and her campaign administration were all to blame. It was this feeling of subtle subjugation that she hated most of all, not her mother, in truth. The hardest part of being the offspring of someone illustrious was their enormous shadow.

The mysterious man looked desperately from side to side. “I can’t come back,” he responded.

Garcia looked over him suspiciously. “Why?”

He ignored her inquiry and continued. “I have a message to bring. Can you deliver it to Katrina?”

Garcia nodded slowly.

“The SGG have found her, and we have come back to reap retribution for her desertion and betrayal. I tried to warn her that moving from California was not the right thing to do.”

Something was odd.

“I tried to warn her; once you are part of us, you can never leave. But she left, and she took the ring too. Why she would steal from her own gang, I will never understand.”

Garcia froze. Did he say *gang*?

“Tell her that we’ve come to take back what’s ours and that we’ll be coming next Sunday. Tell her that the message was given by Victor.”

Garcia remained bewildered. Victor left right after giving the message, leaving Garcia confused and petrified.

*　　　　　　*　　　　　　*

It was seven sharp, and her mom had returned from her office. She hollered a hello to Garcia, but Garcia chose not to reply, as she always did.

Usually, Garcia tried to ignore her mother all day, but today was different; she had a message to give and some questions to ask.

Garcia laughed at herself. Her mother was the mayor of Shire Rock, now a candidate for governor. She was the illustrious Perfect Patty.

Katrina even has her own flag, and her many supporters wave it as passionately as they would the American Flag. Maybe Victor was a crazy person, an inane conspiracy theorist.

Yet Garcia had to deliver the message; it was her duty. Even if this man was insane, Garcia had to at least tell Katrina the message. Garcia took a deep breath and entered the living room. Katrina reclined on the couch while reading an article in the newspaper. She only gave a glimpse towards Garcia, and continued reading. Garcia had a mind to turn around and leave in pure defiance, but she stood her ground despite her rebellious instinct. Garcia wanted to deliver the message, even just to see the look of Perfect Patty's face at the accusation.

Katrina

2

Katrina, exhausted by the pious obligations of a mayor, laid down on the sofa immediately after work without giving a thought to greet Garcia. All she wanted to do was to sit her couch and catch up on a new novel she purchased a while ago. Katrina just recently became an avid reader; where she came from, books were the last thing on her mind.

That day at work was especially strenuous. Being a mayor was hard enough; now, since she was running for governor, she had to find a way to juggle her duties as a mayor and as a candidate. Rhetoric was becoming an irritating obligation than a passion as it once was when her campaign began. Her audience always applauded any word, whether gibberish or oratory. It got increasingly boring; everything thrilled her in the past.

Katrina despised being just a nominee, begging for votes as a hungry man does for food; she wanted to be governor, then president, and finally if the people agreed, Supreme Majesty of the Universe. This desire was new, introduced to her a few years ago, after the great Perfect Patty landslide. However, now it was her sole ambition, her reason for living, the meaning of life.

After engrossing herself in her book, Garcia's presence interrupted her. She approached in an awkward shuffle. Katrina could see that her daughter was trying to keep up with her rebel image, but for some reason, it was a challenge for her to do so. Garcia eventually managed to utter out what she wanted to say.

"A person came by to see you today and told me to give you a message. It was from a group – called the SGG or something."

Her heart stopped.

"They wanted to tell you that they're here to get back what you've taken from them. They're convinced that you pilfered something, a ring, from them."

Katrina didn't know what shocked her more; the fact that they found her, or that they were still out to get her.

Garcia tried to appear indifferent. "The messenger's name was Victor."

Katrina didn't understand how they caught up with her. She took so many precautions to evade them. This was a dramatic reminder of why she hesitated before delving into the realm of politics; she needed to keep a low profile after she moved.

Once Katrina became re-aware of Garcia's presence, she realized that Garcia must never figure out the meaning behind the message. She tried to flash a casual smile to Garcia, to reassure that the message was nothing but nonsense; unfortunately, Garcia noticed the terror in her mother's eyes.

"Mother, you don't know what he's talking about, do you?"

Katrina yearned to tell her daughter to disregard this message as pure craziness, but she felt that she lacked the strength to lie to her daughter's face.

"Garcia, I know very well that I kept this from you for too long now, but I guess I can't hide this from you any longer."

Garcia was bewildered.

Katrina gently patted her hand against the couch. "Maybe you should take a seat."

Garcia glared at her and pouted in subtle disobedience.

Katrina sighed. "I'm going to tell you the real reason why we moved when you were young. Please remember that in the past, things were different. *I* was different. Don't let what I'm about to tell you change your opinion of me."

Garcia finally capitulated and sat down on the sofa. She was less bewildered now, but more intrigued than ever.

"I was involved with certain… *criminal* activities; I was part of a gang. I did shameful things, and I have witness things a woman should never see. That dark period in my life haunts me to this day."

Garcia was stunned; it was as if she was too shocked to react.

Katrina went on. "The reason why I took part in such activity was because I felt trapped, and I thought crime was the only way for me to get ahead. I was ignorant; I didn't know better."

Garcia was already horrified, but her usual tantrum was stalled.

Katrina continued. "I met my husband, your dad, around that time. We hit it off. Soon, he finally proposed to me, and he managed to get me the most beautiful ring. When I asked him where he got it, he told me he just found it. I was too stupid to realize that it was stolen. Or, if I did, I didn't care. I loved the ring so much. I would have died for that thing. Soon, it came out that the diamond on the ring was very valuable; it was worth more than this house! Our gang found out, and they declared that it was theirs. Unwilling to give away the ring, your father and I refused to hand it over. Because of that they killed your father."

Tears ran down Garcia's eyes. She only had a few memories of her father; he died when she was three. She always heard from her grandmother that he was an angel. Garcia never truly got to witness what a great person he was.

"I fled here for refuge, but they found me. They want the ring. I still have it. I have no choice right now than to give into their demands."

After looking into her daughter's flooding eyes, Katrina stood up from the sofa and turned away from her daughter in shame. Soon, she reddened, and scorching tears began shooting down her face. Grief suddenly seized her, and her body began to tremble violently.

"And the worst thing is," Her voice was so miserable that her words sounded like moaning, "I still loved the ring after his death. More than I loved him. It possessed me… even today, I still can't bear the thought of losing it."

She wept loudly for a few moments. She looked at her daughter, expecting to find at least some sympathy. There was none. Then, almost professionally, she got herself together. The trembling stopped, her eyes went dry, and her voice went back to normal.

"I only hope you can try to understand that the past is the past and forgive me for it as well." The tone in her voice sounded strikingly unemotional.

Garcia finally found her voice. "Understand? How can I *understand* that a person can be a thief one day and Perfect Patty the next? How can I *sympathize* with a hypocrite? You *killed* my father. His death was your fault. You are a fraud, a thief, a murderer, a bad mother! Perfect Patty, my ass! "

Garcia stormed out, but Katrina knew better than to follow. All she could do was continue to lie on the couch. She knew that she had to take advantage of any peaceful moment she could get, because her stable life was about to stir up once again.

Maybe the thrill will return, thought Katrina emptily.

Lebron

2

"Kids, I need to tell you something." Charlie tried to say this as delicate as possible. "Miranda is going to go away for a while. She-"

"Is she going to come back?" The innocence in her voice was heart-breaking.

"No, she isn't." said James, pouting. "She's going to leave us just like mommy."

"James, it's not your fault. She just wants… time to herself."

James stood, arms folded, facing away from his dad. "You mean time *away* from *us,* right?" His voice started to quiver. It was inevitable that he would start to cry. "She hates me. It is my fault; I'm a bad son."

"James, you can't possibly blame yourself for this. You're barely six years old! These things are out of your control." Charlie said, trying to comfort him.

"You blame me too. I know it's my fault." He said, sniffling.

"Stop talking nonsense."

"It's my fault she left, like it's my fault mommy left." He began to bawl uncontrollably.

Charlie, caught off-guard, commanded James to go to timeout. James ran away, howling. It was all he could say. He didn't expect James to say any of the things he said. What could he have said? He tended to say dumb stuff when he was at an instantaneous loss for words.

"Daddy, why do they have to leave?" asked Sasha.

"What do you mean?" Charlie said.

"When old mommy left, we were very sad. Why did new mommy have to leave, too?" Sasha said.

"Honey, it's just that-"

"I don't care for her. She was mean. I'm glad she left." said Sasha, sniffling. She left before she could shed a tear.

Charlie sighed sadly, feeling defeated. He saw no need to chase after them, or to move, for the time being. So he just sat there, dejected, trying to think of what to do next.

Later that day, Lebron's father came up to Lebron and James' room, looking for James. When he found Lebron instead, he had an instinct to turn around and leave, but he had to tell Lebron about what happened. As Charlie sat down, Lebron glared at him knowingly, yet coldly. Lebron's eyes told his father that he already knew. Lebron didn't even need to say the words *I told you so*. His father already understood.

Charlie opened his mouth as if to say something, but no words came out. Charlie was a simply atrocious speaker at times and this unpleasant quality appeared at the moments when he needed speaking ability the most. So instead of speaking to Lebron, his son, and ending the awkward silence by doing so, he just walked away.

* * *

A few weeks after Miranda left, things were changing. He was fired from his old job due to downsizing, but he found two jobs in replacement. As far as he knew, Lebron himself was working two jobs to help out. Lebron's father told Lebron him that soon he would be able to go back to school and pursue his dream. Deep in his heart, Lebron was a little skeptical, but he still encouraged his father.

Yet one day, things took a turn for the worst. Apparently, as Sierra was driving one of her friends somewhere, the friend placed a magazine in front of her face to show Sierra a photograph, interfering with her vision. When Sierra pushed the magazine away, a car almost crashed into her car. To avoid a collision, she jerked to the left, but by doing so she experienced another collision. She collided against one of the petrol pumps.

That was what Sierra told Lebron happened, at least. What Lebron knew for sure was that his father was mad. His father had to pay for the damages. The whole neighborhood could hear dad yelling at Sierra.

Lebron knew the root of his anger wasn't due to the actual accident; it was the payment. It always seemed as if every time they got ahead, something brings them back. They were fighting an endless battle, an unwinnable war.

Even though Sierra didn't show it, she took her father's words very hard. The next day, when Lebron went to visit Sierra, all he found was Sasha, crying. Sierra's room was empty. When he asked Sasha what happened, she told him that Sierra just disappeared. She left with everything, even her bed.

She was long gone.

Jack

2

I tried to remember the good days, the days where this road was less painful. I remembered when a kid named Lebron walked this road with me for a little while.

I was still wandering around the Rock. I was ten, and I was tired of living on my own. I was mature, in a way, because I had learned to become independent through my hardships, but I was very illiterate.

After years of starvation and scraps of food, I was ravenous for at least one full meal. I remembered the great taste of pizza, its awesome aroma and the satisfaction it left one with after eating it. The memory of pizza was a faint memory, fading fast, but when I found a pizzeria, to my pleasure, the thoughts of the delectable delicacy came back to me and made my mouth water.

Being uneducated, I couldn't grasp the concept of price at the time, and the menu looked like mere numbers and symbols to me. I found a dollar on the sidewalk earlier that day; I thought I was rich. I asked for a large peperoni pizza, and when they asked me for the $20 I owed, I proudly handed over my 1 dollar bill.

They were about to kick me out when a nice, younger kid, probably eight or nine, bought it for me. He had been given $30 dollars for his birthday and spent most on me. He was about a little over four feet, yet his slender figure gave him the impression that he was taller than he actually was. He had dark brown eyes that were somehow welcoming and short, nappy, buzz cut hair.

Before I could show my gratitude to him and thank him, he asked, "Where are your mom and dad?"

"I don't know." I looked down.

He said, "Look, kid. Follow the red and black Sedan in front of the restaurant. That's my parent's car. At home, I'll figure out what to do."

He went into his car. Its license plate was 1Vass45. I followed his direction and did what was told. Luckily, his parents did not drive fast and they always stop at the stop signs, which were common on the path they took. We ended up in one average, yet nice house. I hid in his bushes until I saw him in the front yard alone.

"My parents are not really generous, so we have to keep you a secret. You could live in our tent we never use. I promise to bring leftovers to you after we eat."

"Okay, but can we play sometime? It gets boring staying in one place." I asked hopefully.

"Okay, but if my folks see us playing, tell them you're a neighborhood friend." He advised.

"By the way," he added, "my name is Lebron. What's yours?"

"Jack," I replied gladly. I had made a new friend. He then told me of his hope for the success of this arrangement and of his enthusiasm to help someone less fortunate.

"That's what my teacher keeps yammering about. That teacher is a hypocrite, you know."

Lebron not only kept his promises, but even went out of his way to perform gestures of generosity to me. He was very charitable and playful during my time there. He went out and played with me every day. He gave me his stash of toys to play with when I got bored. Even though I did not shower, he was not hesitant in lending me his clothes. We were like best friends. Luckily, his parents never noticed me, despite my inhabitance of their tent. It was the best of times, and it harbored most of the greatest moments of my existence. For the first time since toddlerhood, I experienced the innocent bliss and blind happiness of childhood.

The first two months I spent with him were filled with play and joy, for it was summer vacation, and Lebron and his friends played with me endlessly. At the end of the day, his parents would order Lebron to come inside and the kids usually dispersed; I would pretend to leave the backyard for a spell, and then sneak back in when the time was right. After that, Lebron 'volunteered' to take out the trash and smuggle some goods for me to munch on. That was how things went for the summer months.

Once school started for Lebron, the days were lonelier for me. I usually found a pastime, but I always awaited the arrival of Lebron with zeal. After he did his homework, Lebron came outside with books he acquired for first, second, and third grade levels to teach me. He had learned that I was illiterate and had not went to school, so even though I was older than him by one or more years, Lebron devoted time to teaching me.

Though I had been very confused at first, I had caught on very quickly; maybe I was a fast learner from the beginning. After several months of this, Lebron declared that I had caught up to him in education.

Lebron began to borrow fourth grade books at the library and give them to me so I could read them on my own. After doing this for a about eight more weeks, Lebron decided that I could not go one like this and that I need the same quality education everyone else was getting; thus, he proceeded to come up with a scheme to get me into the fourth grade classroom.

I constantly tried to dissuade Lebron from the ludicrous idea time and time again, but despite my greatest efforts, Lebron was already devoted to planning a ruse to breaking me into the classroom. The more I resisted the idea, the more he determined he became in scheming. My opposition was waning as his insistence and his conniving grew. Eventually, I ceased combating the idea; the sneaky conspirator had won, and he began to tell me about his plan.

"Okay. I've come up with the scheme to get you into the fourth grade. Want to hear it?" he asked with enthusiasm.

My uncertainty returned. "I don't know. I doubt that this will work. I mean, isn't there a whole education school system or something?" I inquired.

"Don't worry about that. This will work. Besides, there must be a reason why America is getting beat by a bunch of other countries in learning." he informed.

"Where'd you hear that?" I wondered naively.

"I overheard it when my dad was watching the news."

"Well, yes, but what would happen if we get caught?"

"You don't have to worry about it." He said reassuringly.

"Okay. Tell me the scheme." I demanded.

"Well, I was thinking that maybe if you arrived to the school early, you could sneak into one of the closets and hide there. You will be able to listen to the class and see the board through the little slides in the door. I have already spoken with the janitor, and the janitor is willing to look the other way. We could meet in lunch and I can share some of my food with you then. Deal?"

Reluctantly, I consented. He told me that the plan would commence the week after next.

*　　　　　　　　*　　　　　　　　*

This memory made me feel good for a while, that I had a friend and that people acknowledged me as smart. *Maybe, I could get a job or something. I'm a legal adult now. I can do whatever I want without people asking me for my parent's permission. Probably I could go to college soon.*

Then reality hit me. There was a second, more painful part of the memory, too.

*　　　　　　　　*　　　　　　　　*

I was outside in a beautiful spring day. I was lying on the lawn, playing with Captain America and Godzilla action figures. The front door slammed open out of the blue. I dashed to the tent, afraid that Lebron's parents had come out to survey the backyard. In the tent, I remained silent, waiting for other sounds indicating the arrival of Lebron's parents. Sure enough, I heard sounds of two voices arguing loudly, and footsteps arriving closer and closer. Suddenly, the footsteps stopped, and their shadows lingered over the tent menacingly.

"I think it's about time we get rid of this tent." A female voice said.

"Why should we even bother? It won't cause any harm." A male voice retorted.

"Well, it can attract insects and bugs and spiders and rodents and rabid animals and-"

"I think you're overreacting. You're just looking for a reason to oppose Me." interrupted the male voice, who I assumed to be Lebron's father.

"There you go all over again. You accused me of so many things over the years. Do you think I'm hiding something, Charlie?" replied Lebron's mother.

"Honest to God. I have every right to be suspicious of you. You have been getting out a lot, and I found-" (he whispers something) "in your purse. What was I supposed to think, Susan?" Charlie asked.

"You know what is wrong with you? You lack trust. How could you invade my privacy like that? You know we have two children together and I would not hurt Lebron or Sierra." retorted Susan.

"I don't want to deal with this anymore. I'll check the tent ." declared Charlie.

"Throw it away. It must be filthy by now." reasoned Susan.

Lebron's dad, Charlie, muttered, "Waste of a perfectly good tent" as he opened the tent door to see me there. I was petrified in fear. I wondered whether to run away and never return, or to introduce myself and hope that they were reasonable people. Neither of these seemed like good reactions.

Charlie was just as shocked to see me there, but Susan gave him a look that said I told you so.

Then, she said obnoxiously, "Did I forget to mention strays?"

Charlie just ignored her, and then asked who I was and what I was doing there. I told him that I needed a place to live and had nowhere else to go. Susan grunted and demanded Charlie to deal with the situation; afterwards, she walked off haughtily.

Charlie explained to me that I could not live in a tent, and how that was no way for a child to live. He said that things would have been too complicated for a person like me to live. I partially understood at first, assuming that he would let me stay with the family.

“So does that mean you guys will let me stay here with you?”

Charlie shuffled side to side, looking uneasy.

“Well, we cannot let you stay here. Times are getting tougher, and it’ll be best for you to-” he tried to explain awkwardly.

“Well, I think it’ll be best for me to stay here. I’ll have a home and a family like I’m supposed to, like all the other kids my age, instead of being a vagrant.” I said.

“Well, I’m sorry, but there are other factors to weigh in. I have to pay for a lot of things because of my children. We also have to pay the house, and having a third child would just put more strain on us.” Charlie tried to say this in the most delicate way possible.

“Why am I the only person to have to suffer like this? You complain of bills and financial strain, but how about me? I don’t eat a lot; only a scrap a day would suffice. I could wear hand me downs.” Jack paused, sniffling. “You have it easy. Imagine how hard it is to see other kids enjoying life, getting everything they please, and not giving a damn about anything.”

“Well, maybe you could be put up for adoption-“

“Why? So I would have to wait for other families like you to not adopt me.”

“Calm down, sonny. I don’t want to be mean-“

“But you’re only looking after yourself.” I began to run away.

“Kid, where are you going?” Charlie shouted.

Nowhere, I wanted to shout. If I had stayed, the next day would have been the day Lebron and I would have executed our plan. Instead, after many years of lacking education, I succumbed to illiteracy once again.

* * *

That experience made me realize that life was not fair, and that I walked this road alone. No one else in the world cared for someone like me. I had to toil on, alone, because nobody else knew me.

Suddenly, I got drowsy. I lay along a sidewalk to sleep, uncaring to the disgusted pedestrians surrounding me. As I fell asleep, I silently prayed that the dreams would bring me to a better place.

* * *

A large multitude of people crowded around a building, humming with commotion. The police tried to keep the spectators away from the scene, but the mass grew larger and larger. The bystanders were determined to witness the scene unfold. They watched the suicide bomber stand on top of the building, ready to jump. It was not a terrorist attack, just a suicide attempt. The guy told the police, and the audience for that matter, that if anybody tried to do anything hasty or drastic to get him down, he would ignite the bomb.

After the guy told the audience what he would do, the audience erupted with sudden tumult, mayhem and fear, yet the audience was too stubborn to leave, and too interested to miss how the following events would unfold.

The police shifted their priorities from calming the crowd and keeping the peace to trying to softly and gradually convince the guy to get down and terminating that public hazard. The cops one by one tried to remind him about the great things in life, and the unending possibilities. They told him that no matter what a person had to suffer; suicide was not the proper way to escape them. Besides, you never know what the future holds. But the guy would not listen. He just questioned every move they made. He told them of the bleakness of his life, and how lonely he was. The guy's plight was very similar to mine. In fact, he reminded me of myself. His train of thought was delusional, but it wasn't a far cry of mine. He also wore the same outfit I wore, the filthy rags and leftover bags I fashioned into clothes.

The police force was losing patience for the bomber, and what started as subtle, compassionate coaxes turned into aggressive and blunt commands. Finally, the chief tried to talk to him. The chief was perhaps the most hostile of all.

A rogue group of cops started covertly entered the building and were making their way up to the building. When they reached the top, the suicide bomber took one eerie look at ME. It was freaky, like it was an omen. It felt like I was seeing a vision, a prophecy of my own death.

Then he jumped and activated the bomb, and as he jumped, I suddenly found myself in that person's place, hurling towards the hard, cruel ground. Yet, I also felt as if I was watching myself fall, like I was a spectator in the audience as it grew chaotic with fear.

As I was heading to the ground, the bomb strapped across my chest was ticking its last minute, but fifty-nine seconds before the bomb would have exploded, the chief of police shot me as I was in the air, causing the bomb to explode in the air, harming no one. The chief muttered "piece of trash" and threw the corpse into the trash. To top it all off, the general looked straight at me, with his golden pupils. He smiled, and said "Is this how you are going to go? The sooner the better." He unearthed a laugh so uncurling and evil.

The chief looked all too familiar. I could not believe my eyes. I froze, petrified with fear. A dawn of horrific realization fell upon me. The gold eyes, clean looks, the handsome expression, and the frightening evil tone he had... the general was my demonic clone from my first nightmare, the one who had spelled out the letters of a word that I tried all my life to avoid. He was there, laughing at my imaginary suicide.

Garcia

2

The week before the gang's arrival was the oddest week of Garcia's life; it was if those days were only leading up to something, something dramatic. Things were different than normal. Katrina spent much less time working, gave much more attention to Garcia, and wanted to spend more time with her. Garcia did not know how to react to these changes, but she suspected it was only in the wake of what would come.

Once this is all over, she will go back to her conceited self, Garcia thought, but for some reason, she was not as staunch in her rebellion as usual; in fact, she was very lax in her defiance. Perhaps that was in the wake of what would come as well.

Katrina had tried to calm Garcia, but Garcia knew that she was, in truth, mostly attempting to calm herself. Garcia could sympathize with her in that way; how could she face the gang she used to be a part of when she had changed so much? Any mistake and it could end with her death.

Her mother kept the ring in the storage room, but as a precaution, she placed it in a shelf by itself and labeled the shelf 'ring'. Garcia knew she did not want any mishap, major or minor, to occur and she treated this issue very urgently. Garcia knew that her mom was really worried because of the type of people they were: violent, short-tempered, ignorant, and unwilling to 'play games'.

Once it reached Saturday, she tried to spend the day relaxing with Garcia. Garcia decided not to put on her rebellious attitude that day; it did not seem right for her to spurn her mother before they were about to experience a fearful encounter.

They spent the day at the park, then the pool. At the end of the day, Katrina invited Garcia to recline and watch a movie with her; Garcia thought that was too odd for the relationship they had, but her mother's unusually welcoming eyes won her over.

Then, Katrina asked Garcia to pray with her; Garcia was shocked, because they hadn't prayed together since the night before the first day of middle school. They prayed separately ever since then, though it was very contradictory to their culture.

Garcia's mom held her hand and they started to reverently recite the Our Father. Garcia oddly felt comfort in holding her mother's hand in prayer once again. *Don't get used to this*, she warned herself. *Things will get back to normal soon.* Then, they stated the Nicene Creed, cried the Hail Mary, and shouted the Glory Be and many other prayers. After that, the two warbled several Spanish choir songs. Finally, they uttered their thanks to God and Jesus and afterwards quietly proposed their intensions. Garcia told her Lord her intentions, and her mom did the same.

* * *

The next night, Garcia awaited the arrival of the gang. The day was intense: thick with fear and anxiety instead of the ordinary substance a day was usually composed of. Katrina sat on the couch in front of the front window of the house, and even though Garcia tried to occupy herself, Garcia felt as if she was sitting on that couch all day, awaiting the alleged arrival of that gang. Garcia couldn't do anything that could take her mind off the waiting. Whatever she did to entertain herself felt wrong, because in her gut, she felt as if she should be at her mother's side at the window.

Finally, it was night and Katrina bid it well that Garcia should go to bed. She agreed easily, but a sick churning in her stomach told her that she had probably made the wrong choice. Nevertheless, Garcia took her rest, but it was likewise intense: thick with fear and anxiety instead of the ordinary substance a night was usually composed of. Garcia found no true relief in her respite.

Suddenly, she awoke in the middle of the night to the ringing of the doorbell. Her eyes were already rheumy and she had grown accustomed to her odd sleep, but she immediately threw on some clothes and darted downstairs. It appeared Garcia was just in time and did not miss anything. The gang was finally here.

"Katrina, it has been so long! How are you doing? How is your daughter? How is life here?" said a woman in front.

This woman wore all black attire; she wore a black tank top under a dark leather jacket, shadowy skinny jeans and gray sneakers. She incompatibly had hazel green eyes, brownish-black, long hair and a strong, stiff, tan body. She appeared young on the surface, but underneath, signs of age abided.

Garcia's mother remained silent; she didn't come here for small talk. She spoke to this woman through her eyes while her expression was kept stiff; the eyes told the woman *get to it!* . The woman just beamed.

"Get on with it, Benita." muttered on of her goons.

Ignoring him, Benita continued in her deep Mexican accent. "You remember Victor and Romero? Of course, you do! Can you imagine that we have been apart for around ten years! That's a darn shame."

Katrina just stared at an unrecognizable, Oriental face. "Who's he?"

"Aye, I almost forgot. We have a new recruit! His name is Alexander Khan." Benita's smile grew a little more uneasy.

It was obvious that Victor and Romero were twins. Victor was the color of light ebony, but Romero was slightly lighter than his brother. Their appearances were almost exactly alike and you could not tell them apart if it was not for their hairstyle and apparel. Victor bore braids on his hair of flawless proportions, not too long, not too tall, not too many, and not too little. Romero had a Mohawk: maybe six inches high and about one or two inches wide. Other than his Mohawk, Romero's head was filled with small stubs for hair. They wore suits of different nature, Romero's colored red, streaked with black stripes, and studded with shiny black diamonds for buttons; Victor's was a plain white suit with black streams. They both appeared to be having a youthful attractiveness.

Khan was the most mismatched one of the gang. First of all, he was tall and burly. His skin was pale with a yellowish tone like parchment, but his hair and eyes were black. He looked like the youngest of them all.

"Katrina, remember the good old days. When no one would mess with us and we got everything we ever wanted. When we did whatever we wanted and never got caught. When we silenced our enemies once and for all." said Benita.

"You mean by killing them!" Katrina stated courageously.

Benita was taken aback. "Don't tell me you forgot how things used to be, Kati Kat. We had to do what we needed to do. This is a dog eat dog world. Our ghetto back home is no different. In the business world, people will do anything to get money. In the political world, scandals and lies rise in order to attain the supreme authority. The whole world follows the same principles, but it is just shown in different ways depending on the part of the world you're at."

"Many people lived long and peaceful lives in our neighborhood without having to resort to criminal activity. We were idiots, too foolish to seek honest ways to survive. You're nothing more than a couple of thugs." Katrina said confidently.

Romero spoke up this time. "Kati, don't mess yourself up with your high class interpretations of what goes on down there. Those interpretations are fairytales told to rich people to appease their guilt. They believe it so they can be morally allowed to condemn and demean us. They do this and say that we mess up our own lives to the point that helping us would be useless. And you know who told the rich people all the fairytales?"

"Shut up."

"Look, lady. We don't want to start any problems. We just want the damn ring. So are you going to hand it over or not?" said Khan impatiently.

"Relax, Khan. We have plenty of time." said Benita reassuringly.

Khan bore an irritated look on his face. He kept glimpsing at the window uneasily. "No, we don't actually. The McGinley clan is on our tail."

Benita's smile, that Garcia had grown used to, disappeared into a frown as she muttered a silent "Damn." Then, she looked at Garcia's mother and stated, "Give the ring to Khan and we'll be on our way."

The confidence that Katrina had vanished and she nodded stiffly, paralyzed with sudden fright. She speedily dispatched Garcia to retrieve the ring.

Garcia did what she was bid, going down into the basement with fear lingering around her. She tried to calm herself through the skillful use of inhaling and exhaling deeply, but fright was always nearby, despite her most vigorous attempts. As she entered the basement, Garcia swore she saw a figure in darkness sneak away through the back door, but she reasoned that the apprehension was getting to her. Garcia then boldly resolved to not let the fright faze her, but as she examined the empty drawer, terror coiled around her throat and gave a fatal squeeze. The ring was nowhere in sight.

Instinctively, she did a cursory search of the basement, but no ring was found. After crawling on the floor for a desperate hope of finding the ring, she decided to capitulate to her misfortune. She dutifully made her way upstairs, but each step was heavy, like a convict's on death row.

"-doesn't show herself in ten seconds, I swear, I'll-" Romero stopped in mid rant.

Katrina gave her daughter a look with trusting eyes, as her whole facial expression loosened with relief. Almost joyously, she said, "Garcia, you are finally here!" Katrina gave one final glance to Benita and the others, and announced grandly, "Garcia, please hand over the ring."

Garcia, guilty beyond record, just shrugged sheepishly, staring at the ground. She could not imagine what she could say in a moment like this. *I am going to get in big trouble when all this is over,* Garcia told herself.

"Garcia, this isn't the time to play games. Give them the ring!"

Embarrassed, Garcia walked over to her mother to tell her the unfortunate truth. She never forgot her mother's sudden shift from smile to frown. The once trusting eyes her mother bore were now wide and panicky, and her mother's expression hardened to the point of no return.

After she stiffly turned to face the group, Katrina tried to awkwardly explain what happened. It was the first time in Garcia's life that she heard her mother, the great orator and speaker, stutter.

Benita laughed heartily, as if what Katrina said was too ludicrous to be pondered, but her fellow gang members did not perceive the apparently obvious hilarity of the moment.

Romero had a look of disappointment, with traces of disgust. He had his arms crossed together, as if to say "well, well, well, look at what we have here".

Victor seemed more sympathetic than his twin. He frowned guiltily, gave her a look of sorrow, as if to say, "I would do something if I could". He looked away, already hit hard by the damaging grief and distress that would follow.

Khan, however, showed little emotion. The little emotion that was shown was, weird enough, a kind of readiness, adrenaline perhaps. It was as if he was eager to know what would happen next, and what he would have to do.

"Kati, it is a mystery how you make me laugh. Hand it over for real now." said the gang leader.

Katrina started to tremble and the smile on Benita's face disappeared.

"Benita, we were home girls. I will not believe you would play such a trick on me as a pathetic attempt to usurp what is rightfully ours."

"She is not lying; mom is telling the truth." Garcia blurted out, to an adverse effect.

"Tick, tick, tick. To get your own daughter involved in such dangerous business, what kind of heartless women have you become? Grab the girl." Their leader ordered.

Khan made a sudden grab for Garcia, but luckily a knife flying from the hand of her mother stuck the man's chest. An inch to the left and she would have hit his heart. During the distraction, Katrina revealed her hidden gun and commanded the ruffians to freeze. It all happened so fast, yet Garcia always remembered it all in slow motion. Katrina extracted her weapon; Benita ducked, then Romero made a futile attempt to reach for his own gun; Katrina, ready to fire, realized the bullets that zoomed past her. They were discharged from a van parked outside the front yard of the house. Suddenly, the bold, gun-brandishing Katrina collapsed, revealing Victor, wielding his own gun, an old fashioned rifle with a frontal spike that could have easily substituted for a sword.

Vomiting blood, Garcia's mother squirmed on the tiled floor, silent except for difficult gasps. Garcia's astonishment violently stabbed her heart and she herself had trouble inhaling the simplest of breaths. She could have easily fainted right there if not for fear that in her moment of weakness she could also have been shot, like her mother. Garcia thought that she would prefer being shot than suffering the state of mental chaos she was about to undergo; besides, the shock was more excruciating than any bullet could be.

"Why Victor, why?" Katrina choked out in between hurls. She tried to use the bipedal legs humans were blessed with, to no avail.

"I have changed a lot since you fled my friend." he admitted. "I am not the weak pushover you once knew."

Katrina went into a small coughing fit, blood spurting out of her mouth, her body suffering an inhuman quake. However, she managed to utter, "I never thought you were weak; I thought you were someone who gave from the good of your heart, but I see that you have lost that quality and became one of *them!*"

Victor, suddenly stricken with the sick realization of his deed, dropped the gun suddenly; he glared at the hands that committed the crime, as if he could not comprehend what they had done.

Katrina was barely accomplishing to survive when the van outside the mansion opened, revealing an armada of well-armed mobsters.

"Damn it. The mob tracked us down. Finish of Kati and her daughter, NOW!" screamed Benita.

Katrina told Garcia to escape as the Mafioso's weapons began to discharge. It, by no competition, was the most terrifying moment of Garcia's life. Bullets flew everywhere, raining explosives ubiquitously and everything transfigured into one violent shatter. It was the most underrated battle in history, and no safe haven was to be found. Inevitably, Garcia snapped out of her hopelessly daze and was ushered into a hopelessly desperate faze. Unable to think clearly, she irrationally made a dash to the back of the house. The gang was too busy to notice her escape, but nothing seemed to be safe. Only one thing was safe to assume: Katrina was dead. Her body fell down once again as the shooting started, but her difficult gasps ceased. It would have also been rational to expect that her corpse was shot to smithereens during the gunfight.

Stupidly, Garcia ran upstairs to retrieve some items before her eventual departure. Once inside, she locked her door, and packed furiously. A gunman soon rammed down her door, obviously looking for valuables, which would have included witnesses. Before the person had a chance to shoot, Garcia abandoned her things and made a seemingly suicidal leap out of the window, falling to the ground in pain. No time to moan, Garcia thought to herself, only to run. Once she broke through the gate that surrounded the perimeter of the property, she sprinted; and sprinted; and sprinted.

Garcia ran until safety was guaranteed. At an intersection, Garcia noticed a woman in a 2009 Alfa Romero 8C Spider, admiring some sort of small shininess she held in her hands. Suddenly, Garcia recognized the figure; it was the same person she thought she saw in the storage room. An eerie realization came over her; that woman was the one who stole the ring. Garcia suddenly recalled the open window she neglected to notice right then. The woman's clothing was all black, and with her already pitch black skin, she was the human equivalent to a shadow.

Another realization soon succeeded the first: her idiocy ruined her life and, even worse, caused the death of an innocent person, her mom, who reached out to her and trusted her. Garcia was ready to beat herself, and the thought of suicide was not distant, but she knew it would have solved nothing. As the woman of darkness rejoiced over her prize, Garcia was filled with a vengeful rage. Almost instantaneously, the answer became clear. As the Spider began to ignite, Garcia began following the car.

Garcia had to re-obtain the ring from her. She began to pursue it in A Chase like No Other.

Jack

3

There have been several incidences where I only proved to be a burden to those around me. The most painful example of this was the memory of Maxwell, Joey, and my run-in with the Mafia. In retrospect, the whole experience seemed cinematic, but every moment was accurate.

Then, I was a gritty, maturing adolescent,. I knew that I walked this road alone; my gun was my only companion. It was not loaded, but I kept it around for the intimidation effect. I had to resort to a predatory way of life. I told myself that I had to do what I had to do, and that if I was not clever, this world would eat me alive. I never thought that I would be dragged back into relying on another family once again.

I remember meeting Maxwell; he was with his friends and cronies, but when his companions had to leave, an older adolescent, I guess about seventeen, came up to him, grabbed him by his collar and held Maxwell up against the wall. I sprang into action, and told the adolescent to leave the kid alone while I flaunted my weapon. The adolescent glared at me, and asked me if that gun was loaded. I nodded, trying to look tough and intimidating. But when he took out a gun of his own, I made no attempt to appear threatening or dangerous. I did not know what he was about to do next, but I suspected that he would either try to scare me off or shoot at me. But before he could make a follow-up move, five cracks rang in the air as the stranger fell to his death. Behind him was the kid he was harassing, looking at the body, emotionless, apathetic and indifferent, while holding a gun of his own. I was bewildered at not only his deed, but also his possession of a fully loaded gun himself, and his apathy towards this guy's death. Maxwell introduced himself, and advised me to be ready to not only wield a gun, but to use it too. He was about my age. He asked me where I lived, and I told him I did not live anywhere. He brought me over to his dad's house, where they offered me a job.

"Kid, I hear you saved my son Maxwell from a goon from the Winter Hill Gang; is that true?" asked Maxwell's dad.

"Yeah." I replied.

"I also hear you are in possession of a gun. Do you know how to work it?"

"I guess so." I said.

"Listen. I'm the Patriarca Family's top recruiter. This is my son, Maxwell. We don't usually recruit people without getting to know them, but this is an emergency. Someone's been snitching to the FBI, and a major part of our forces have been either jailed or killed. I have a hunch that it's someone from the Winter Hill gang that's been snitching, but nobody hears me out. I need you to be a gunman. You'll get housing in a mansion, where you will be treated. Call me Joey." He said.

I was not sure at first; I needed a home, but I felt uncomfortable with the killing business. With their motives so unclear, they look like a bloodthirsty, but sophisticated killing organization. Still, the streets were no place for me to live.

"I'll take the job, but I-"

"You do not have to be nervous, son. I know how you feel. On my first day, I was a wreck. But look at me know, I'm at the top of the family! You'll fit right in." said Joey reassuringly.

Maxwell spoke a lot about his dad; Max said that his dad was the best person in the world. Maxwell would go out of his way to show his dad his accomplishments in his training. Every time his father acknowledged him, I felt empty, excluded and a little envious. Something about Max and Joey's father-son relationship made me feel like I was missing something. Every time I saw this phenomenon, I was motivated to do better at the training, so I could be acknowledged by Joey one day.

However, sometimes Joey did not have enough time to spend with his son, and sometimes Max pestered him because he was so busy. It really saddened him. Once, he overhead Maxwell crying privately over his dad. I never understood him.

Basically, "training" was done in a large room with large counter-like furniture where different types of guns lay. They were labeled and organized by accuracy, quality, range and other characteristics. Apparently, other people came to practice. In the front of the room, there was a large and wide mechanism. When turned on, elaborate dummies of your enemies appear. A target sign was strapped to each, and you had to shoot them down. At level two, they would shoot at you with water guns while moving around. It was like a carnival game, except this was more elaborate and fancy.

On the side, there were some bloody arcade games that freaked me out due to their graphics. The main purpose of the arcade games was to desensitize us enough so we would feel comfortable killing people; it worked impeccably for Maxwell, who was addicted to these games. It never worked on me, though it was said that those games were five times bloodier than the Call of Duty franchise, with a lot more killing.

I was surprisingly good at training; I did not think I was so great, but everyone else acted like I was a homicidal beast. Max was a little irritated due to all the attention I was receiving, but I was too naïve to realize it then. Training a junior mobster at first seemed like a class dedicated to bloodthirsty murder, but then it gradually got more enjoyable. There was not as much pressure, and it gave me a weird sense that I was becoming a normal kid. I mean training was similar to those arcades you see on TV, except every game was weapon-related. As with me and Maxwell, we were sort of friends; yet there was something that kept distance between us, as if there was a wall separating us.

As I excelled in the training, Joey started to acknowledge me and placed much of his pride in me. Joey said that I was like a son to him and that I would always have a place in his heart. He started to make more time for me out of his schedule and once even declined a contract because he wanted to spend the time with me. For a while, I enjoyed the comfort of a fatherly figure.

I should have realized by then that he spent more time with me than he did with Max, his own son. As I got closer to Joey, I was exponentially distancing with Max. It was intentional; Max was for some reason avoiding me. I didn't mind and still considered him as a friend, but every encounter got more intense. He gave me the occasional act of hatred that told me that something was wrong between us. However, I refused to think that we ceased being friends.

Maxwell and his friends, who were also mobsters, used to arrange a yearly competition. I wanted to join the competition, and apparently Maxwell has won every battle since they started to execute the competition. We had to use paintball guns with red paint to represent blood. However, I convinced myself that because I was a mobster-in-training, I needed to act the part.

But Max glared at me, smirked and remarked that even though I had 'a knack at shooting things up', it took true authentic aptitude for one to win the competition and that I didn't have what it takes. I responded defensively, saying that shooting things up was the main point at being a gunman. I also added that I was not sure he knew what he was talking about. However, Max did not appreciate my comment.

His friends told him that I had just insulted him, or that he wasn't going to take this and should fight back. He asked me if I was challenging him and I shook my head. I knew that he was about equal to me, but I submissively told him that he would surely beat me. The last thing I wanted was to lose him as a friend. He smiled and told me that I better remember that and that, even though I was inferior to him, that I was allowed to take part in the competition.

The object of the competition was to hit someone on three of their vital spots; once someone's three vital spots were shot, the person was out; the goal was to be the last one standing. There were uniforms worn, marking the three vital spots focused on: the right lung, the throat and the heart. I had the smallest paintball gun; I learn that this one shot bullets fast, so I did not care. Because of this, they thought I would lose.

First round, I eliminated two people right at the start. I then ducked, ran and hid behind a rock. A guy tried to jump the rock to get somewhere, but did not see me, so I took advantage of my opportunity. I hit his spots so quickly that it took him a while to realize that he was exterminated.

Round two, only four were left. I went to a dark alley to hide. I waited a while, and then some sucker was trying to shoot someone while he was in front of the alley. I got him, but he still did not see me, so he was confused.

Last round, just me and Max facing off. I wished him luck, but he just glared at me, his eyes like a tiger that spotted his prey. I started by shooting him once fast, then running to the nearest hideout. I took out his throat, and he recoiled. I went in the same alley, but I noticed a fire escape ladder that led to the roof of the mansion. First, I shot a mirror so it could ricochet off it to confuse Max of my whereabouts. After that, I climbed onto the large gutter. I edged my way to the front to see Max running towards the other end of the street. I waited till he came close and knocked him down. He was so shocked and tried to shoot back, but I already won. His friends cheered me and made a big fuss over it. Maxwell gave me a dirty look and disappeared into the house.

A few days later, I was going to go on my first mission.

A rival crime organization was going to rob a bank. With the money, their leader would go into hiding and possibly flee the country.

The objective was to get the money, and to kill their leader, a man named Whitey Bulger.

The mission involved Joey, Maxwell, countless other armed mobsters, and I. He was fleeing the area, and it was probably the last chance we had of getting him. Max was not so thrilled to learn that I was coming, but he did not fight it.

Everything went as planned at first. The enemy successfully got away with the money, leaving town square in a state of chaos. The robbers had armadas to escort them safely out of the crime scene. We waited on Vick Street until they arrived. The street was flooded with limos and armed men on foot. Max and I were the youngest ones in the battle. The Rival Mobsters were surprised to see us so they tried to run the other way. The road was empty of everyone else except mobsters, we made sure of that. They tried to turn around, but we were shooting them down. In a few seconds, most of the walkers were dead, and the battle was done on wheels. I did not want to actually kill someone, so I just sat quietly in my limo. The money, Joey said, was not in a car, but was being carried around in an extremely insulated safe. The person holding it was in the middle of their unit, wearing a bulletproof outfit.

Maxwell was standing out of his window, shooting maniacally and psychotically. He was not making any progress. Suddenly, he began throwing explosives with terrible aim. Instead, one of them hit a large oak tree. It fell on top of some cars upfront. Needless to say, the road severely blockaded. The enemy almost got away.

Joey, in a fit of rage, grabbed Max and started screaming at him at the top of his lungs. He went on about how the mission was practically ruined, and how important it was to the survival of their organization. He had his hand in a fist, ready to hit his son. He hesitated at first, but his frustration continued to boil hotter. He backhanded Max hard across the face. The power of the strike made Max crash against the side of the car. The hand print on his face wouldn't disappear.

While Maxwell lingered on the verge of tears, I got an idea. It might be risky, but it was worth a shot. A while ago, I learned about circuits and electricity. If I could hit the fire hydrant, causing it to spew water all over there, and some how manage to fracture the support of the high voltage wires without severing the wires themselves, maybe it would send a shock that would electrocute the walking mobsters while causing the limousine automobiles to burst into flames.

I got a high range gun and shot the fire hydrant closest to our fleeing enemies. It quickly spewed water all over there. I then shot down the support for those high voltage wires nearby. I tried not to actually cut the circuit, which was hard from long distance. When the wires fell to the water, a shock of electricity sent their cars exploding and flaming. My plan worked exactly as I wanted it to.

Joey, almost bipolarly, began to dance with joy. He began to congratulate me fervently, and began to shower me with compliments and praise. He even offered to make me his right hand man.

But the one thing that stood out for me was when he called me his son. I was shocked, but touched. I didn't remember how the love of a father felt. I realized I found a new family.

But this thought was short-lived. As I stepped out of the car for a breath of fresh air, Maxwell began to reload his gun. He had another battle to fight. He followed me out of the car. I turned around to see a stone faced young criminal with a gun point a gun at me. His finger was on the finger. He whispered, "Die, brother."

But before he could fire, I sprinted off. He tried to shoot at me at first, but the bullets strayed all over the place; he never had good aim. He started to chase after me. I crossed the street towards small, outlet store, made of hardy stone and brick. I tried to get inside for safety, but I tripped. Quickly, I tried to get up, but before I was halfway, I saw him at the other end of the street, walking contently in my direction, gun raised. He discharged one bullet, and the crack of a gun was followed by the screams of the wounded.

I lay there, bleeding, almost sure that I was dead. But the bullet did not hit me. I was not the one that screamed. I turned around, horrified to see Maxwell, on the floor, squirming violently on the floor, cussing passionately. I suddenly realize that the bullet ricocheted off the stone brick wall behind me to kill him.

Max soon took his last breaths. By the time Joey came, his son was dead.

Joey took a look at his deceased son, and then a look at me. He knelt by Max's limp body and embraced it. He began wailing outwardly, and then glared at me with an icy cold hatred.

"Bastard! You killed my son! Bastard!" He repeated this over again as I ran away. My once loving fatherly figure now wants me dead; he mourns for his real son.

There was nothing else to do except to flee. And that was exactly what I did. I just ran and ran without stopping until I was sure I was away from them and swore that I'd never come back.

Lebron

3

Lebron looked around, nervously and impatiently. They said they would be here already. It was dangerous enough for him to rely on them, but this deal has gone on for months now. Nevertheless, Lebron was just as nervous as the first time they encountered. Lebron knew better than to trust these goons, but he always found himself behind the Angleton's West Branch Library, awaiting the arrival of their arrival. He stood against the wall, trying to look nonchalant about it, but he trembled terribly. Why does he continue to make appointments with Ajax?

Every other week, Lebron met with the leader of a notorious gang called the Glocks. They were just a group of hoodlums who got wealthy off of crime. There were six of them. They had connections with most of the local gangs and criminals. In the city's crime world, they were the de facto enforcers; they helped those who were on their good side, but eliminated those who defied them. Their leader was known as Ajax.

Finally, he came. Lebron's thoughts had quieted. Ajax approached him.

"Hey, Ajax. How's …stuff?" Lebron shuffled awkwardly from side to side, too frightened to look at Ajax.

Ajax was surprisingly young for his position of power in his gang. He was about Lebron's age. He looked around gloomily. "Not good. The cops have been really cracking down on us lately." He sighed. "A couple of our brethren have been caught and we have been trying to pay their bail, but it's hard to maintain the throne of being a drug lord if we have to spend the money on bail. Times are tough." He paused and added simply, "I got to get paid."

"Oh, I'm very sorry about how things are going." He approached Ajax to comfort him, but hesitated. "I never knew that these times were even rough for crime lords." Lebron chuckled clumsily after the comment, trying to ease the mood. His attempt failed.

"I understand things are rough, Ajax. If there is anything I can do to help, let me know." Lebron said. Lebron suddenly felt sick. What could have possessed him to say such a thing? He could have gotten himself involved into something illegal, let alone dangerous. He started to tremble again, but only lightly.

"Well there is something you can do…"

Lebron's uneasiness returned.

"Do you think you'll be able to begin to pay us back soon? I mean, we could really use that money now."

"Well, Ajax, it would be hard for me to pay you back for all you guys did. I mean, I'm barely carrying on as it is."

"As I said before, times are tough. I realize that things must have been hard on you, but we have been very generous with our lending, even raising the amount of money we're giving you. And for what? We need this money."

"We need this money too. You've got to understand, Ajax, that I cannot repay this debt. At least not now."

"No, YOU need to understand that we need this money more than you do. If I go broke, so does a lot of other brothers. You've got to understand that I have a lot of people's backs. I can't abandon them. I have to provide for them. The Glocks are my family. I live in a public orphanage that feels like the penitentiary." Ajax's once friendly expression hardened.

Lebron's shuddering grew more intense.

"I can't pay you back. There's no way. We have enough problems on our plate. The last thing we need is more debt. So-''

"We?! Who is this 'we' you keep talking about?"

Lebron froze.

"I thought this deal was between you and me, kid. Is there someone else involved too? The other gang members don't know about this. If they find out..." Ajax paused in worried contemplation. "Who is this second person?"

"Actually, there's more than just a second person."

"What! How many people are there?"

"Other than me ... four, maybe three." Lebron managed to choke out. *He's going to kill me*, Lebron told himself.

Ajax stood menacingly over Lebron. He reached into his back pocket and revealed his weapon.

"You brought your gun? Why?"

"What's it to you? Who are these other people?" Ajax pointed the pistol at Lebron's forehead. "Well? I want names, now!'

I knew it; he is going to kill me! Lebron thought to himself. Lebron could not think, and started to panic. His trembling intensified to the point that his extremities moved spastically and lost the ability to move.

His vision blurred, and his mind went reeling as he felt the world spin around him. Lebron was having a panic attack.

He finally shouted out desperately, "It's my family!"

Ajax grimaced in rage. He loaded his gun. He placed his finger on the trigger. "Ungrateful…"

"No, no, no. I'm serious. The reason I asked for the money in the first place was because we needed help. I want to pay you back. I will. Just not in the near future, man. Trust me. I put in on my life."

Ajax lowered the gun. "Do you realize how dangerous it is to owe a crime lord money?"

Lebron nodded.

"You'd go that far for your family?"

"I bet you would go that far for yours."

Ajax went silent. Lebron also stood silent. The two both realized how similar they were, despite their different lifestyles. At that moment, the two knew that they would become perfect friends if willing. They both could understand each other and share each other's pain. Maybe friends that close could make life bearable.

But they could never be friends. It would never work, and it would endanger both of their families. Besides, they weren't brave enough to do so. Maybe they could be friends in a perfect world. But this was not a perfect world, and they each had their own paths to take, but soon fate would pit these two against each other.

"Never mind." Ajax mumbled, and with that he left.

Lebron did not receive any money, but he knew that his deal with Ajax was over. He was not going to get paid anymore. Lebron could not bear to break this to dad, so he decided to keep this to himself and maybe look for a job. At least one component of his stress was gone.

*   *   *

Charlie had to get an extra job and do extra shifts. Lebron was the babysitter while he was gone. His father applied for online college, so he took his classes in the morning. During the day, Charlie worked from 10 am to 7pm, then to go to his second job at 10 pm to 3am. Lebron's father would sleep till it was time for Lebron and the others to wake up and go to school, which was 6:45 am. This would be his routine for weekdays. On weekends, he would take online courses for three hours. Then, he'd get called to work for someone, and he'd go. Charlie eventually ended up spending four consecutive hours with his children on Saturdays, but on Sundays five hours (if you include church).

The major downside of this was that Charlie always had to leave the twins alone. Even though Lebron watched them often (with and without dad's knowing) there was still a significant amount of time that they were home alone. This started to have a deep affect on them.

Apparently, throughout the time they spend spent alone they became scared of something they thought was the boogeyman. At school, whenever an unknown sound sounded, they would both scream and hide in the nearest corner. Apparently, it had been a big problem at school. The teacher also told Charlie that both of the twins seem to be troubled deeply. He has been trying to find out why.

*   *   *

"Lebron, you know that it's not right for me to leave these kids home alone. It's dangerous. I need to stay at home and watch the kids. I have to watch the kids when you go to work. Maybe I could quit one job." Charlie said.

"No. If anything, I should be quitting a job. Or both if I need to." Lebron replied.

“Lebron, I couldn’t ask you to do that. The more reasonable decision would be for me to quit.” Charlie said.

“Dad just let me quit my jobs. I understand that times are tough and that we have to take the initiative. You don’t have to shelter me. Hell, I would quit school-“

“Lebron, you realize that we need *your* paychecks to keep us running. They’re a large chunk of our money.”

“Dad, you are the father. Your paycheck is more important than mine. C’mon dad you don’t have to quit.”

“Lebron, stop kidding yourself. I know that your overall paycheck is larger than mine. I do not understand how you get paid more than I do, but I know that your paycheck is most of the family’s earnings. The day you quit both jobs is the day we become bankrupt.” Charlie said.

But I’m not going to come home paid anymore. Lebron wanted to say this to his father. In fact, Lebron wanted to explain the whole situation about Ajax and his generosity. But he kept his mouth shut. Suddenly, Lebron felt as though he needed to vomit.

“Another option is that I could convince someone we know into watching you guys for the time being. You know, until we get back on our feet.”

“How are we going to do that, dad? Our relatives are hundreds of miles away and you don’t have any" Lebron froze in the middle of his sentence, wishing he could take back what he said. Charlie stayed silent, but he got the message. Charlie did not have any friends close enough.

Charlie was not an outcast or sociopath. In fact, he was far from being a sociopath. Charlie had many friends in his golden years and did not have one enemy. The issue was that Charlie was unsuccessful compared to his friends. While Charlie fell in love, got married, enjoyed his honeymoon and produced his first child Sierra, his friends were working hard to become successful, leaving Charlie in the dust. His friends became high class, rich and successful, yet he was, in a way, lower class compared to them.

His nearby friends were not very close, so he does not talk to them much. Probably, they were the type of people who talk of their riches and their freedom from children and family. Charlie was the exact opposite of these people; in this case, opposites do not attract; he hates people like that. He was an all out family man.

His closest friends moved far away and were always visiting exotic places, plus Charlie was too busy to keep in great contact with any of his friends. Once, Charlie planned to surprise his friend on his birthday by visiting him. He planned everything: Charlie would take a train; stay at a hotel room that he booked; and show up at the surprise birthday party that his friend's relatives informed him about. By the time he got there, his friend was on his way to meet an illustrious author in China. The surprise party was cancelled, but no one told Charlie.

No one ever told Charlie. Charlie always felt unfairly excluded from his former companions. It was as if they had a problem with him. Charlie does not care. If they had a problem with him, they should confront him about it. Maybe they think that they were better than Charlie. It seems this way also. If it was this way, Charlie was not going to pretend that they were best friends. Charlie has tried to ask them why, but they reply with answers of naïveté and innocence.

Now, Charlie always envied his friends, in a way. He was a great student, went to college, graduated college at the top of his class, went to university, passed university with high marks and had a carefully planned, bright future ahead. Something went wrong along the way, unfortunately, and soon Charlie found himself trapped in the working class. Even though he worked harder, studied more and got higher grades than his friends, he became a 'nobody' while his friends became 'somebodies'. 'We live in a hovel,' Charlie sometimes said, 'and we still are struggling to pay the bills.' Yes, Charlie has some envy for his friends, but he would not trade lives with them if he had the chance. He loved his family too much, and in the end, he was not complaining.

Charlie had to sacrifice his dreams for his family, but he adopted a new dream, a dream for success for his children. If his children grew up right and had a future, his new dream would be fulfilled.

Charlie sacrificed his social life for Lebron, Sierra and the twins. He has no time to himself, only time to provide for the family. Time was money, so since the family was short on money, Charlie surely was not going to spend time on anything irrelevant.

"I'll find a way." said Charlie. It was an odd phenomenon when parents say that, because when they do, the parents usually find a way, most of the time in a secretive manner, or they neglect it completely, in some cases.

"Maybe I could pay a babysitter to watch over the twins."

"No. I think it may be too expensive. You should not even consider it."

"But their safety is all that matters." said Charlie.

"Dad, I know our budget inside out. There is no way for us to pay a babysitter regularly. Please tell me you aren't considering this option."

"All I wanted to do was to look over my options with you."

There was a moment of awkward silence.

Finally, Charlie told Lebron that he was free to go.

Lebron knew that the budget has become too dependent on his paycheck. He also knew that he would not be in this mess if he actually tried harder to look for a job instead of taking the easy way out. He knew that he screwed up badly, and that there was almost no way to fix it. Lebron went to his room and buried his face in his pillow, wishing that he would suffocate. Maybe crying would get the job done, Lebron thought as he cried silently, his face in his pillow.

* * *

One day, when dad was at work and Lebron was at school, the twins thought they saw the boogeyman. They said they saw it on the sidewalk through the window. James decided to fight off this 'boogeyman'. James wandered on the street looking for it. Sasha called 911 using the home phone.

As Charlie was driving home, he saw James walking along the sidewalk, lost. Charlie picked him up and when he got home, he found a lot of police cars around his house.

The cops needed to have a word with Charlie. At the end of the discussion, the police decided to let him off with a warning. If this happened again, James, Sasha, and Lebron would be taken away from him.

When he asked James why he did so, James told him about the 'boogeyman'. Charlie told him that it was the most ridiculous thing he had ever heard and that he always told James to be careful and stay safe. "You're never home to protect us, so why should we listen to you?" James snapped at his dad. Charlie was wounded deeply by James's words.

* * *

He woke, rheumy and still tired, as usual. Lebron clumsily made his way into the living room to greet his father. Stumbling down the stairs, he found himself eavesdropping again, because what he saw was shocking in itself. His mother and his father sat on the couch, obviously deep in conversation.

"Huh, you guys manage to keep the house without me. I'm surprised you aren't getting evicted. Did you pay the mortgage in food stamps?" She said smugly.

"Why do you always have to-" his father paused, taking a deep breath to calm himself. "I did not invite you over so you could mock me. I understand you owe me a lot of money worth of child support. If I had a right mind, I would sue you out of triple the money. But, because of my nice nature, I decided to work a proposal." his father said peculiarly.

"Like you have the guts to do that! You're strong in most ways, but your fat heart is your weakness. You might as well - "

"I would seriously be considering being very nice to me right now. I know what you've been doing, Susan. I knew it since the divorcing stage; I know what your sister has been doing." His father said strongly.

She said nothing, but opened her mouth in horror. She slowly put a hand over her wide opened mouth. It was as if Charlie found her kryptonite. He could have done so many things to wreak revenge upon her or blackmail her in the least.

"My proposal is this: be a mother to your children. I can't take care of them on my own, and you of all people should know that. That's all I want you to do. Baby-sit, visit them, do whatever a mother should do. That's all I ask."

His mother looked at him worriedly. The smug, annoying woman turned into a concerned and worried one. "Do the kids really need me? Were they really that distraught since the divorce?"

"Yes, and the second divorce didn't help either."

"Well, I can't do it. I'm sorry, but I have a life of my own now, a house of my own, husband of my own, a *family* of my own." She said, rubbing her belly.

"You mean you're…"

She nodded. "I did not expect you to call me over here, but I simply can't do it. I don't have the time anymore."

"You must have some free time. Come on; I'm desperate. I'll even pay you." He said, as a last attempt.

"Really?"

"Yes." He replied.

"How much?" she asked with a newfound curiosity.

Lebron, watching what was happening, could not suppress his anger any longer. He did not yell at his mother, or even his father. He yelled at him far too much. He was tired of that. He just gave them one glare, and stormed out of the establishment.

Lebron felt as if he lost all respect for his dad. Couldn't he see that she was going to leech off of him again? Lebron did not know what to think anymore, or who to trust. The mother he loved treated his father like dirt; the father he used to respect was a blind fool. The rational Sierra threw all caution to the wind, diving into something she barely knows. *We are in worse shape then than I assumed,* he said to himself.

Lebron walked out on the porch to see his mother's nice car. *She's rich,* Lebron said to himself, *that's why she would not help us anymore. Her life is as comfortable as it could be while we suffer.* He took one look at the car, and vehement passion told him what to do next. A sledgehammer lay on the side of the street, tempting him to wield its destructive wrath. The same cruel Fate that manipulated misfortune into his life just to spite him encouraged him to wield that sledgehammer.

All reason and good judgment left him. Lebron wielded the sledgehammer and devastated the vehicle. He was relentless as he was foolish. He began with attacking the windows, and then advanced to her tires. After finishing with her tires, he gave one strike to the trunk of the car. It opened with a bang. Inside, Lebron found a gallon of gasoline. Lebron sprinkled the gasoline lavishly over the car's engine. He took two rocks and tried to make a spark, but after a while of trial and error, he impatiently threw the rocks on the ground. Instead, Lebron just hit the engine with the sledgehammer. He never saw a more beautiful blaze. The blaze itself was not bringing Lebron pleasure, just the feeling of revenge felt so… right to him.

A guy on the street froze as he saw him hammering the trunk of the flaming automobile. He stood still, afraid to move, and put his hands up as a sign of surrender.

Lebron ignored him; all Lebron wanted was justice, one way or another. He did not care whether his definition of justice was morally correct. Yet Lebron chose the easiest way to attain justice. He was finished, but he gave one last glance at the devastated auto, and noticed something glistening in the trunk. In the trunk, he found many things, but what caught his eye was a beautiful ring, with a diamond worth millions.

"Oh my God, what the hell happened to the car?" his mother shouted. Then, she took one glance at Lebron, who was already sprinting down the block.

She unearthed a truly terrible screech.

Then and there, on the morning to remember, the chase like no other began.

Garcia

3

An automobile with no roof was a criminal's dream. Foolishly thought to be stylish, it allows the perpetrator to have easy access to all the materials in the car, thus facilitating robbery and theft. Garcia regarded herself as no criminal; in fact she was disgusted with them. But this was also a retriever's gold mime as well as a robber's.

Garcia followed the pitch black Spider until it stopped in a parking lot of a motel. The woman then disappeared into the motel. Garcia, finally able to utilize the opportunity, ravaged the vehicle for the ring.

After searching every inch of the auto, Garcia realized that the woman probably had the good sense to take the ring with her. In her pure frustration, she let out a yell of distress. Then, she realized that the investigation was not a complete loss; Garcia uncovered some objects that would be useful in her quest for vengeance.

Garcia examined the materials that especially caught her eye: a GPS, a sleeping bag, a knife, and a miniature handgun. The last particularly intrigued her. What could she possibly need a gun for? She was no bum; she was the daughter of the would-be governor. Garcia was taught, raised, and knew better than to do so and stoop to the rank of those in the lowest social caste.

Yet something continued to engross her about the gun. It promised a protection that she would need if she was serious about pursuing the robber. Besides, who was she kidding? Her mother was dead. She had no relatives that she could remember, nor friends close enough to house her. She was on her own.

Garcia decided to keep all these items, even the gun. Her stomach grumbled, and her legs ached in agony. She turned around to see a simple solution right in front of her: the motel. Garcia decided to stay there, not caring that the mediocre name could signal mediocre quality.

The hotel's outdoor architecture was awfully standard, yet the interior design of the motel was far more attractive than the exterior. The walls were mostly crystalline white, with traces of glitter. Decorations plagued them though, ornaments unifying with ribbons, streamers likewise collaborating, and paper chains and posters installed a treaty, all to form one unstoppable coalition. All were cheesy, especially the posters, which presented a witless play on words, or lousy pun, with a visual to represent it. One poster Garcia found really appalling as in originality was a cartoon of Uncle Sam, with a caption saying *God Bless America! ... For KB&R!*

She approached the front desk, labeled customer service in bold. The clerk was a middle aged woman with dark orange blonde hair. Her features glowed pinkish peach and barely contained any wrinkles. Her facial expression, however, looked stiff. She smiled a smile that appeared to be photo-shopped onto her face, because underneath the seemingly generous smile was a hard-hearted smile, obviously an obligation. Garcia felt a little bit queasy, and anxiously pulled out her mother's debit card she found in her pocket.

"Greetings, fine customer; How can I help you?" she said softly.

"Can I stay here for the night? Nothing fancy, just a one bedroom room with a bathroom."

Examining Garcia closely, disbelief portrayed itself on the woman's face, as if she could not believe Garcia made such a request. Barely taking a glance at the board that labeled which room was occupied and vacant, the clerk made a showy 360 swivel with her chair.

Then, she informed, "I am sorry. We have no rooms available at this moment."

Garcia looked behind the customer servicewoman to see the board behind her. About half the rooms were free.

"Is room 217 available?" Garcia inquired casually after noting which rooms were not taken.

"No. I am deeply sorry for the inconvenience." She did not even turn around to confirm her reply.

"How about room 133?"

"No rooms are available at this time." The woman declared firmly, with a barely noticeable shade of irritation. "May I offer you a discount for your next visit?"

"I can see the board from here." Garcia told her, losing her temper fast. "Why are you trying to prevent me from acquiring a room? I have a debit card." Garcia handed over the debit card to her. The customer service clerk gave Garcia a cynical stare after she scanned the card.

"So your name is Katrina Hernandez?" she asked skeptically.

"Honestly, that is my mother's name." Garcia said irritably.

"What is your credit card number?"

Garcia shrugged.

"The last thing I want to do is start any disagreements, but this is a respectable business." She paused, as if to ponder over a probable excuse. “Do not mistake this as any allegation, but I am afraid, due to the great possibility of credit theft, that you must vacate the premises immediately.”

Flabbergasted, all Garcia could reply was a hostile and loud retort. “I am no thief!”

“Please return when you have an adequate and eligible payment source before I have to do something drastic.”

“-like calling the police?”

The service woman recoiled at Garcia’s harsh reply, but managed a weak nod.

“So you assume I am some sort of hooligan? Is that so?” Garcia paused. “I’m the daughter of Katrina Hernandez for your information and if I don’t get the respect I deserve you will most definitely be held accountable.”

“I apologize, but unless I see genuine identification-“

“Damn your genuine identification. Do you automatically assume a person of my appearance is a criminal?”

She was obviously taken aback by Garcia’s statement, but replied calmly yet coolly, “I am shocked that you would make such an accusation. You are simply a suspicious character and I must ask you to quietly exit this reputable institution.” She said more forcibly.

She was about to call security when she noticed something in Garcia’s jacket pocket.

“Do you mind telling me what is in your pocket?”

Then, a sick realization fell upon Garcia: the handgun still resided in her pocket.

“None of your business!” Garcia blurted out.

The statement sounded more juvenile and youthful than Garcia intended it to be. As Garcia's hands shuffled in her pocket to try to hide the weapon, the woman, despite Garcia's attempts, spotted the gun and let out a shrill gasp. Garcia exited the motel swiftly, leaving the woman free to call the police.

*　　　　　　*　　　　　　*

Garcia ended up sleeping in a miniature forest behind a church. Having nowhere else to sleep, Garcia rationalized that a true monster would harm her near a church of any kind, and she felt a, though small, comfort in knowing that God's home was nearby.

Yet Garcia could not get to sleep because of the guilt that lingered. The thought of her mother's nurturing nature that she had taken for granted depressed her could have made her weep for days. She remembered all the time she spent with her mother, and this was the only time in her life that she had appreciated her own mother. Garcia was disgusted with herself. How was it that she finally realized what she had once it was gone?

Her own stupidity, the stupidity she had only several hours ago, similarly appalled her. Why did she spurn her mother so, even when she tried to reach out to her? Even this last week, she held back when her mother's love continually flowed upon her. Her former behavior was incomprehensible now; Garcia remembered odd feelings, perhaps envy or intimidation? They had something to do with attention and her mother's success, but surely it did not justify the way she rejected her mother.

What had she expected her mother to do anyway? Garcia had never thought of that before. *I am a spoiled brat,* she realized. Garcia was launching one, long, irrational tantrum with her mother. Look where that led her. Her mother worked hard to get where she was, and was Garcia expecting her mother to resign just because a couple of blind sheep decided to make her their new Sheppard? The ridiculousness of it all made Garcia distraught beyond imaginable.

The only way she felt she could justify herself was through finding the ring; the pursuit of it became her obligation, her passion, and her mission. That was the only way Garcia could avenge her mother and redeem herself. She would stop at nothing to make sure that golden circular strip made of gold encrusted with a jewel larger than itself was hers. Her mother had died because of that ring which was rightfully hers. The least Garcia could do was to retrieve it. But could a ring really redeem her? Could it really avenge her great mother's soul and eradicate the shame Garcia brought upon the both of them?

Garcia shivered, not only at the thought but also at the cold. The forest darkened as Garcia feared the existence of wild creatures, especially wild dogs and bats, because they were predominant in the area. Eventually, Garcia put her fear aside and shuffled into her sleeping bag.

If only Garcia realized what she had before, if only this epiphany happened earlier, she would have treated her mother the way she deserved. Her mother died with the memory of an ungrateful bastard who sealed her fate with a shrug and a whisper.

Then, it all made sense. She needed to make things right. She was a worthless piece of trash. All she was good for was bringing pain, as she did to her mother. So was it not justified that she inflicted pain upon herself? Yes, the holy, piercing pain of a knife would do the trick. It would be logical for her to strike her wrists, just so she could monitor how much damage she received, relative to blood flow. *Yes, only a madman would not understand this, because it makes perfect sense*, Garcia thought to herself.

But first, she needed to be tried by a jury. Justice clearly emphasizes that someone was innocent until proven guilty. The sylvan environment became a court, the rocks and branches its jurors, one mighty oak the judge. The prosecutor, a thorn bush, presented its case flawlessly, and impeccably convinced the jurors that Garcia was guilty. Garcia had no defendant attorney and simply and audibly agreed that she was guilty when interviewed. Her mental jury found her guilty of murder.

Garcia was sentenced to a nightly slashing of the wrists.

Lebron

4

Lebron stopped to take a breath after sprinting a mile from the scene. He sighed. Why did he have to destroy the car? What was he going to do now? He realized with horror that his dad would have to pay for the damages, which was ironic, considering she owed him thousands in child support. He wouldn't be able to face his father, or his siblings. The only person he knew who could help him through this situation was Sierra.

Luckily, Sierra told Lebron her address a week after she left. The apartment building was nearby. He was in desperate need for advice; maybe his sister could help clarify his options. Lebron knew she would always have time to spare with him.

He took out the black bag in his pocket and scrutinized the ring inside. Why did he even take this thing? However, as he held it in his hand, he grew attached to the pretty spectacle. A thought occurred to him; it might be worth something.

Lebron arrived at the lofty apartment building. The establishment was insipidly named My Place Apartments. On the outside it was the uniform gray of most buildings, and within the establishment the colors were chiefly sepia-based. The lobby was not as impressive as the height of the building, but it was adequate. The entrance to the apartments had a security lock. Lebron foolishly tried to knock, but the lobby clerk advised him to buzz in. After doing so, the security lock was lifted, as if by magic. He entered the elevator, the interior was also sepia-based, and there was no elevator music to lighten the dreadfully dull atmosphere.

Once Lebron reached the third floor, he waited as the sluggish elevator doors opened. The apartment numbers were white, but still lacked radiance. They were also rather miniature, so Lebron took a long while finding the apartment number 375. Victorious in reaching his destination, he knocked on the door.

Sierra opened the door, beaming once she perceived Lebron's face. She greeted him ecstatically, and made a hospitable gesture inside the residence. She convinced him to sit on the couch, and inquired him of his hunger. He declined the offer of refreshments and thanked her for her compassionate benevolence. After she humbly replied to the expression of gratitude, the conversation started.

"Hey, bro! It has been so long since we last saw each other! I was starting to miss you."

"I was too. How are things going around here? Tell me everything."

"Well, I spoke to the landlord and it seems that he didn't really care that I didn't have a cosigner. He just wanted to know if I could pay for it. I could, but as a precaution I took a job here, so my rent is at a discount. Things are ok. How about you?"

Lebron hesitatingly told Sierra everything that had happened since her departure, leading up to the present. When he told her of his collision with vandalism, her eyebrows rocketed as high as they could travel.

"Dad must be searching all over town for you. Go home and face your punishment. You'd get in big trouble, and you might have gotten dad in trouble also, but that is the best advice I can give you. What were you thinking anyway? You of all people should know not to do something like that. What could have possessed you to do such a thing?" she inquired dramatically.

"I was really angry. I didn't think. I feel sorry, but how can I go home with this hanging over my head?" Lebron said sadly.

"Dad's an understanding guy; he'll understand. You'd get in big trouble, but dad will still love you. He'll try to protect you no matter what. You're still his son and he will always love you." She said solemnly.

"Wow. The answer was so simple. Thanks for the great advice." he said gratefully.

"So are you hungry?" she asked once again.

"I already declined your offer."

"Come on!" she insisted.

"I am a little hungry, I guess." Lebron admitted.

Maybe this whole experience was a wake-up call, thought Lebron to himself. He probably needed a drastic personality change, or at least a new perspective on life. This was probably for the best. His family may not be wealthy, but as long as they stayed together, things might turn out all right.

Lebron opened a cabinet in Sierra's kitchen in a quick search for food, but instead he found a couple of plastic Ziploc bags; they were filled with a green herb. Lebron took one and walked to the living room.

He gave it to Sierra, confused. "What is this?"

When she didn't answer, he finally realized what he was holding.

"Weed?"

She looked away from him in embarrassment.

"Sierra, why? This stuff's illegal! How could you-"

She interrupted him abruptly.

"Can we talk about this outside? I don't want anyone to overhear." She whispered.

Lebron was already charging out the door by then. She followed him out. Lebron had no intention of staying. Yet Sierra brought him to a halt before he had the chance to.

"Please let me explain."

"I don't need an explanation. You're smoking. What other explanation is there?" Lebron snapped rapidly. He was losing his temper fast.

She sighed.

"When I ran away, I couldn't find a place right away. I was homeless and had to crash at my friend's house. I was regretting my decision, but I couldn't go back home. I am too much of a burden. So, one of my friends invited me to a party to ease my stress. At the party, everyone was doing it. She made me try one. 'This will help you unwind'. I didn't want to try it at first, but then I took one. And it did help." She paused. "Don't get the wrong idea. I'm not a big smoker. It just helped me through a tough phase in my life." She said slowly, looking at Lebron peculiarly.

"Now I have a good apartment, better grades, and a well-paying job. And I've stopped." She said this looking at the ground sheepishly. She also stammered a little bit, just like when she told dad about what happened to the car.

Knowing Sierra, she did not act in that manner unless she was hiding something. Suddenly, he made a connection.

"What about that car accident? Were you *high* then?" Lebron accused. Her eyes widened with shock at the accusation, but she did not object.

“I know you are lying, Sierra. I know you better than I know myself. Now, I don’t know what to believe. Were you really ever depressed? Or were you just CRAZY for those expensive anti-depressants?”

She stayed silent once again. Lebron never before knew the power of silence, nor how much it could reveal. He never knew that silence could be so shocking, enraging, provocative, yet revealing. In his case, it revealed who Sierra really was, a weak person.

After a moment of intense silence, she sat down suddenly and buried her face in her hands. She must have felt embarrassed, and that everything she has done has been all for nothing. She must be thinking that she has lost Lebron’s respect. She must have feared that he would not respect her anymore. That she will forever be a burden to her family. That she always managed to make things worse. Lebron knew these thoughts were running through her mind.

Her body started to tremble in a way that confirmed that she was sobbing. Lebron, who ran out of patience, just looked at her with glaring eyes.

He could not believe what had happened to his sister. Where the host of a strong spirit stood and was transformed into a weak child. He does not know his sister anymore. What had happened to staying strong, holding your head high, facing adversity head on? The Sierra he knew would have helped his family move forward, instead of holding them back.

Lebron stood there, the feeling of anger prancing inside his body, feeling of melancholy lingering, but hopelessness was always nearby. She tried to explain and whatnot, but he was not listening anymore. He realized that his whole world fell apart, or was in the process of doing so. Lebron could definitely not show his shamed face at home, but where else would he go? He did not trust Sierra anymore. Who else would he go to?

He finally told her that he yearned for some solitude. Sierra looked at her younger sibling with tear-stained and still watery eyes, and made one last attempt to make him understand.

"I never wanted things to be this way. Neither did dad. No matter how hard we tried, pain comes our way. I guess we're cursed. I tried my best and I wanted to help the family.

"You know me, Lebron. You know I wouldn't do this intentionally to hurt you. You know I love you all. Things are messed up. I know that. You know that I spent my time trying to make things better. Why does any of this matter? Does a couple of blunts or pills, change anything?"

She was tearing up once again and was about to break into a sob as she gave Lebron a last glance.

She stood up and went inside her apartment building, dejected. He never saw his sister the same way again.

Garcia

4

Garcia awoke her buzzed, overwhelmingly numb self. She groaned loudly, and as her brain began to revive, she realized that the inadequate sleeping condition had taken its toll. Her whole body endured the same excruciating ache, and her mind was experiencing an exceptionally profound migraine, and her sluggishness was refusing to vacate her system. Her rheumy eyes were closed shut. Surprisingly, her rest was not a bad one though, despite her subpar sleeping arrangement.

Finally finding the strength to stand upright, Garcia lethargically rose and stretched her still lazy arms and legs. She decided to go inside the church to wash up, but washing her face was the only real hygiene she could commit to due to her recent restrictions. Feeling good enough and almost presentable, she collected all the things she had with her and stuffed them inside the sleeping bag, afterwards rolling it up.

Suddenly, she noticed a slight irritation in her left wrist; when Garcia looked down to inspect it, she suddenly distinguished many slits and incisions. Instinctively, she started to panic; what if a creature attacked her during the night? Could she have Rabies or something? She reached into her pocket to call her mother; maybe she could help.

Then, she realized that her mother was dead, and that she abandoned her phone in desperate haste to vacate the premises. Another realization dawned on her that gave her an inkling of relief: the creature who caused the incisions in her wrist was her own self. She slit it the night before. She did not bother to think in depth over last night's cutting frenzy. Almost subconsciously, however, she retrieved the knife from the ground where it laid and brought it along.

Garcia felt surprisingly well and sane for a person who just underwent a traumatic experience merely a day ago. Her mother's death was set aside for something more ambitious: the acquisition of the ring. She seemed less troubled, and she felt as if she somehow took the edge off the otherwise devastating situation. Who knew her mind's constant rankling could be solved by a nightly cutting?

As she realistically analyzed her options, she realized that she only had two: to return to the motel to stalk the lowly thief, or to just turn herself into the police. The one thing her mother neglected in her administration was to bring a homeless shelter to the town, but Garcia doubted she cared much about the poor to install one.

She chose the first, concluding that the second option would always be available, but the first had a fast approaching deadline. So Garcia set out to the motel, praying that the woman was still there. Luckily, the woman was, so Garcia had a mind to simply leap into the Spider, stay hidden under all her rubbish and hope that she would not notice that a person was hijacking her vehicle.

Yet Garcia was born with a better sense, and the opportunity was gone anyway. The woman exited the motel, got into her 8C Spider and zoomed away. As Garcia began to lose hope in the vehicle vanishing in the distance, a cab zoomed conveniently by. Garcia, giving up on her sensible side, leaped in front of the taxi. After the driver braked violently and exited the car to curse her, she demanded a ride. That was the perfect moment for Garcia to be having a gun handy. Brandishing the weapon, she ordered the taxicab driver to chase after the woman's Alfa 8C Spider. He gave in to Garcia's commands.

The driver, however, did not take the situation as seriously as Garcia had hoped. He merely shrugged as she wielded the gun and continued driving nonchalantly. Then, the casual talk commenced.

"Hello. So what brings you here on this fine high-speed chase?" He asked sarcastically.

Garcia scowled and tried to ignore him.

"On our recent survey, stats show that most hijackers choose our high speed services after a robbery. Any thoughts?" he asked in another attempt to comedy.

Garcia was not in the mood. She was already queasy just wearing a gun, and now that she was putting it to use, she was outright terrified. She could not let the driver know, however. "I am in no mood for small talk. Just drive."

"You don't have to be pushy just because you are keeping me captive," he chuckled at his witty response.

"Don't you realize that I am holding a weapon?"

"Yes, and I congratulate you on your success in the realm of crime. There is a discount on fiends under twenty-one."

"Do you take me for a joke?" Garcia replied swiftly.

"Well, if you are a joke, you aren't a funny one. Chill out. At least tell me your name."

Garcia's attempt at intimidation failed miserably, so she gave into his demands.

"Garcia. Garcia Hernandez."

"Hello, Garcia. My name is Carl Andros, but you can call me Andy. It wasn't so hard, was it? It was certainly better than threatening me again, don't you agree?"

Soon, they eased into a full-fledged discussion. Something about Andy's personality was easy to talk to. Andy proved he could pursue a vehicle in a high speed chase and keep an interesting dialogue going at the same time. After conversing about everything from sports to politics, Andy said, "It seems we talked about every single thing except ourselves. Taxi drivers are nosy people, you know. Why don't you start by telling me why you are here? What is a person like you doing chasing after a random car?" Andy asked Garcia.

Garcia sighed. "None of your business. Besides, since I could ask you the same thing, why don't you start by talking about yourself?"

He chuckled.

"Okay, I'll start off. When I was in high school, I was very mischievous and rebellious. You see, my dad is a police officer, so when I got into freshman year, people started calling me a nark as soon as they found out. Everybody, my friends, my classmates, my peers, mocked me.

To wear off the nickname 'nark', I started to do pranks, vandalism, and many other forms of mischief. I was soon known for my hilarious acts of misbehavior, my way of rebelling against authorities and sticking it to my old man. I think I hit rock-bottom when I did this prank that was SO ridiculously BAD. I spray painted all the walls at school, and on them, I wrote very… *profane* things against the establishment.

I did this prank to finally eliminate my rep as a nark, but all it did was get me in major trouble. The school expelled me, my friends hated me, and my dad was so pissed off that he sent me to boarding school for the rest of freshman year and sophomore year.

So, when I got back to my old school, I became a more respectable, good student. I started getting good grades and got into college. Now, I have this job to pay the rent, but I have bigger things in mind for my future." Andy then gave an expectant look to Garcia. "Now, it is your turn."

Garcia smirked haughtily. "I don't have to tell you anything. My life is my life."

"What? I poured my heart and soul into that story and you can't give me even a general idea at what is going on?" he said playfully.

"It is not my fault your life is an open book."

"Come on. At least give me hints or something. What could possibly be so private, huh?" he said in a convincing tone.

"Alright!" Something about him was so hard to resist. "I'm not a wanderer, but I am technically an orphan. I'm on a mission. A mission that requires-"

"What is this super private *mission* of yours?" he inquired.

"I'm tracking someone down. I need to keep on her-"

"Is that the person I am following now?"

"What do you think?"

"I think you need to elaborate a little. Why are you following this person? What are you planning to do once you find the person?"

"I'm going to retrieve something, something important. So, anyway-"

"What is this important thing you want so badly?"

"A ring, only because-"

“So you mean to tell me that you want to steal a precious ring from an innocent woman, I presume, and I’ve been driving you around on your criminal errands?”

“No, I’m not stealing, I am taking something back. Besides, she is as much an “innocent woman” as Al Capone. I am not a burglar, Andy; I am a retriever.”

“So you had this ring, and this woman stole it from you?”

“Not only that, she also contributed to the death of my mother. It was mom’s-“

“So you’re on a quest for revenge I presume?”

“Yes.”

“How did she contribute to your mom’s demise?”

“Well, it sort of was my fault too, but-“

“So you aided in killing your own mother?”

“No, not at all. You see, mom had a deadline to hand over the ring to a crew. So this woman swoops in and steals it without anyone except me knowing. I thought I saw something but I didn’t know for sure. Well-“

“So it was unintentional?”

“Well, I was in a kind of a rough patch with my mom and I am honestly not sure anymore if it was or wasn’t intentional.”

“So those goons killed your mom because she didn’t hand the ring over?”

“Yes. That is exactly what went down. I’m-“

“So you’re out to get this woman.”

“Partially, yes, but-“

“Are you packing heat?”

“What do you mean?”

"I mean are you armed with your clip or something? I noticed that the gun was not loaded."

"I don't know much about handling a gun, or hijacking, and such, but what I can say is that you better not piss me off."

He gasped in a sarcastic and fake manner, but honestly he reacted to Garcia's secrets with nonchalance. He might not have even cared that she was along the border of criminal activity.

"Who are these goons you talked about earlier and what did they have to do with your mom?"

"My mom was part of this gang, but after getting a ring from my father, who they killed, she fled. Unfortunately, they found her and wanted the ring."

"So did you ever get to know your father?"

"They killed him before I was even a year old, but from what my mom says he is an angel."

"What was this 'rough patch' you had with your mom?"

She stayed silent. *I don't know.* Despite her hardest attempts to conceal them, several burning tears darted down her face. She wiped at them furiously.

"It seems like you love your mom a lot, enough to embark on this adventure. Don't take it too hard. It is not your fault." he placated.

His consolation worked, and her tears ceased. Suddenly, Garcia realized she had squealed the whole story to him

When Garcia realized this, she said, "Wait a sec, you squeezed everything out of me! Jerk! It wasn't your business."

"I am sorry, but I warned you that taxi drivers were nosy people. Anyway, it isn't my fault your life is an open book." He smiled.

Soon, the Spider parked in a drive way and the thief came out of the car. Garcia told Andy to drop her off at the curb. They said their farewells and Andy gave her his card as a final jest, saying, "Tell your friends that Andy's car is always there when you need a cab to hijack."

He told me I could call him any time for a free ride. He gave me his number and left. *This is it,* Garcia thought as she crept toward the auto.

Jack

4

This memory only proved to incline me towards the suicide option. But I had to face the truth: I had no life. I lived a vagrant, predatory lifestyle; I did what I need to do to survive, and by doing so, I found myself sinking to low levels in the ranks of morality and dignity. I had to trudge on, trying to survive to see the next day. My life was a voracious one, one of many transgressions, violations and felonies.

The only question was why? Why did I want to see the next miserable day of my life? The longer I lived, the more I suffered, the more others spat in my face, and the more others suffered as well. I had no life, nothing for me to look forwards to, only to dread. Why did I go out of my way to survive?

* * *

The wind blew cool air, giving me a spine-tingling chill, but it was momentary. I noticed that the structure, type, and quality of homes varied on location. In the more urban areas, there were very few houses, mostly apartment buildings; the houses that you would find, however, were new, radiantly and beautifully colored houses. These properties were usually divided into three, as in three homes. Upon sight, you one might mistake them for a local business place instead of homes. Usually nearby, vagrants such as me linger around, holding signs of desperation like: **WILL WORK FOR FOOD! , DONATIONS PLEASE!,** or just plainly **FOOD, SHELTER.** They didn't verbally ask for money, but they seemed to stay around the same place. Cars would pass by them, and the only glances given to them were the sympathetic looks of a child, or the disgusted look of an adult.

Then, there would be a slump between two urban areas where one would find dilapidated and derelict apartments. There, teens commonly sat on or stood around the porch, hanging out. Some fools drove by scared because their phony looks of intense intimidation, which they did purposefully, as a jest.

Then, there were the common people's houses. Their houses maybe a little run down but overall, the people there were average. There were your rich people, your average class and the working class, those barely able to keep up with their suburban lifestyle. Every once in a while, a new house was built, probably every couple of years or so.

I walked up to a fast food restaurant, hungry and ravenous, with my gat ready to flaunt. It was a mediocre business day by my measures: two men horsing around in one booth, another booth with a woman, eating alone, while an elderly woman ambled slowly to her table. The cashier was a male, around 15. I stocked up my confidence, tried to get ready, and braced myself, for I was about to rob the place.

*   *   *

"Nobody move! This is a stick up!" I shouted.

"Hey man, calm down. Why don't you go rob another place that's having a better business day?" the cashier suggested.

"Shut up! I'm not playing games with you!" I retorted.

One of the guys in the booth got up and walked towards the other side of the room.

“Sit down. What do you think this is? It’s a stick up! Nobody move!” I said loudly.

“Well, I’ve got to take a ****.” says the guy.

“Well sit down! I told you, it’s a stick up!”

“Well, I’m not motivated enough to sit back down,” replied the guy. “Aren’t you forgetting something, Mister Robber?”

I realized my gaffe: I forgot to extract my gun. “Is this what you mean?” I flaunted my gun around. Only the elderly woman seemed frightened. The cashier appeared to be moderately shocked, but the woman eating alone was altogether apathetic. The other guy in the booth stood up, smiling.

“I chose a good day to bring Anne.” He pulled out a gun of his own.

I stood there with my mouth open, shocked.

“Isn’t it actually more dangerous to wear a gun to protect yourself rather than remain unarmed?” the cashier inquired.

“That’s what *they* say, but I don’t believe it. I always pack a gat to protect the three things I love the most: me, myself, and I.” the guy with the gun said.

“But it can be known to provoke people; it would cause more trouble than it’s worth.” The cashier argued.

“SHUT UP!” I bellowed at the top of my lungs, trying to regain control.

“YOU shut up.” said the girl eating alone. “I didn’t come here to be in the middle of a stick up orchestrated by an incompetent robber, and to hear two guys argue over the use of a dumb gun!”

“She’s not a dumb gun! Her name’s Anne.” The guy with a gun added.

“Seems like someone’s a little angry.” said the cashier to the girl.

“SHUT UP!” I tried to holler.

“Now what happened, sweetheart? Why are you so cranky, darling?” The elderly woman asked the teen girl eating alone.

“Well, I’ve been stood up by my boyfriend, but when I passed by his house to ask why, I caught him with another girl!” she replied mournfully.

“Aw. Poor baby.” The elderly woman consoled sympathetically.

“Boohoo! Cry me a damn river, why won’t you?” pronounced the guy with the gun.

“SHUT UP!” I declared once again.

“I remember the days when the robber gave a certain amount of respect to the victims, and vice versa. It was consensual. The way you’ve been handling things, sonny, no wonder you’ve lost control of this stick up!” cried the old lady to me.

“SHUT UP!” I repeat desperately.

“Is ‘shut up’ all you can say? What do you want anyway?” asks the cashier.

“Food!” I demanded.

“Wouldn’t it be wiser to get the money? Food here rots quickly.” The cashier replied.

“Whatever. Just give some to me!” I screech in anguish.

“How much?” inquired the cashier.

I stopped to think up a large amount of money, a sufficient amount that would support me for ages. “Everything.”

“Everything? Alright.” He looked into the cash register. “We have about five hundred here.”

“Five hundred?” I was about to be rich.

“Five hundred cents.”

Which was more, cents or dollars? I thought about it for a while, then I concluded that five hundred was a large number, either for cents or dollars.

“Give it to me.” I commanded hungrily.

“Alright.” said the cashier casually. He placed a green bill on the counter. On it was a number, perhaps the fifth, some words and other markings and symbols. I glanced at it first with confusion as I tried to comprehend it, and then glared at the cashier in disbelief.

“What are you playing at?” I yelled at the cahier.

“That’s five dollars.” He said nonchalantly with a mocking tone.

“And where have you been?” said the guy with the gun to the guy who had to go to the bathroom.

“I was at the bathroom, taking a ****. I don’t care what Robby Mc-Robber-Pants tells Me.” replied the guy who went to the bathroom.

“I’m right here!!” I shouted.

“I know.” said the guy who came from the bathroom.

“Take another step, and I’ll blow a cap in here!” I bellowed.

“What does that mean?” inquired the old woman.

“It means he’ll shoot his gun.” replied the lonely teen.

“I’ll never understand your new-fangled slang mumbo jumbo.” said the aged woman.

“You know that this is a real gun. I can shoot anytime, anyone of you!” I threatened.

"Why don't you shoot me? If you won't do it, I'll do it myself!!" said the lonely girl.

"Is that thing even loaded?" asked the cashier.

"Of course it's not. Isn't that right, sonny? I remember in my day robbers had capability. Now, any bimbo off the street can try to rob a place." reminisced the elderly woman.

"Well, I'm sorry things are different now than they were in the 1800s." said the cashier.

"Is that supposed to be some kind of insult, mister? You're supposed to give respect to the elderly! What ever happened to chivalry? It's been replaced with lust and greed." retorted the elderly woman.

"You know what? I'm tired of this. Finally, I can test her out. Anne, it's time for a workout!" shouted the guy with the gun.

"Are you some sort of maniac?" said the cashier.

"What does that mean?" stated the guy with a gun.

"He called you stupid." The teen girl said blandly.

"Why do you say that?" solicited the guy with the gun.

"You're dumb. You name the gun, threaten people openly with it, and are eagerly trying to get into fights with it, and you never used a gun before?" said the cashier in disbelief.

"Do you name a baby after you change its diaper? I think not." replied the guy with the gun.

The cashier rolled his eyes. "It's not the same thing. First of all, that gun is not even alive and-"

"She's more alive than you'll ever be! Now shut up before I practice Anne on you." He looked at me. "Now, I'll count one to ten. By ten, I'll start to shoot. One-"

He aimed the gun at me.

"Two," He put his finger on the trigger.

"TEN!" He started to shoot while laughing maniacally.

I jumped out of the window and managed to scramble away from the scene. When I ceased running, I sat down on the sidewalk and wept.

*   *   *

I saw a bag on an apartment building's porch. Near it, a young guy was talking to an older girl who bore great resemblance to him. I snuck over to the bag. In it, I spotted a diamond, worthy of millions of dollars. I stared at it hungrily, pondering over whether or not I should steal it. Maybe it was what I needed to get back on my feet.

Suddenly, my clone appeared, his voice haunting yet vividly alive in my head. Then, everything started to spin, and my eyesight began to blur. Soon, all I could hear was his voice, and it was hard for me to see anything.

You worthless piece of trash! Why don't you kill yourself already? You know you have no life.

No, I won't. I will not kill myself.

Why? What'll you gain? Why do you continually go out to survive if you have nothing to live for? You're abandoned by your parents, living off scraps, eat from the trash, unknown and neglected by society, to the government you don't even exist, you're stupid as hell, and you can't even rob a fucking fast food joint. Why are you dying to live if you're living to die?

I stood there, defeated. He was right. There was nothing for me to live for.

Look, there's a dagger over there on the sidewalk. I put it there. Stop stalling. It needs to be done.

The spinning suddenly stopped, and I spotted the dagger he spoke of. Then, everything else in sight was distorted, and all I could see clearly was the dagger.

Suddenly, a tiny flicker of hope drifted into my heart.

No. If I take the ring, I could cash it in and become rich. I'll have a life.

Yeah, right. They'll never take it. You won't be able to cash it in. You'll be thrown in jail, most likely.

I won't be. I'll make up a story and they'll take it. They will give me the cash.

So you're telling me that you're being reduced to a greedy robber? This is exactly why you should just stop yourself and kill yourself. I never knew you were so foolish. Come on.

I felt something in my left hand. I look down to find myself clutching the dagger. I tried to let it go, but I realized that I lost all control of that arm. That possessed arm suddenly attempted to stabbed my throat with the dagger. I grabbed onto the dagger with my other extremity.

Stop it! If you won't do it, I will. said the evil clone.

No. I'm taking the ring. I'm taking it and I won't kill myself. I'll have a good life and I'll prove you wrong.

Yeah, stop fooling yourself. I know you don't have the guts to do it, so take the easy way out.

I'm going to do it whether you like it or not.

Make a damn decision. I know you won't steal it.

Watch me. I took the dagger, threw it as far away as I could, and took the ring, walking away from the dagger slowly.

You've made the wrong choice. I'll leave you alone for a while, but I'll be back. You'll go mad, mad I tell you! And it'll all be because of me.

You are going to suffer more and you will see me, mocking you. You will kill yourself. One day, you will!

His voice stopped talking to me, just when the teen saw me with the ring.

"You stole my ring." he shouted as I ran away. He swore, and then sprinted after me.

Lebron

5

Lebron plunged his arm into his pocket, and pulled out a ring, one so exquisite, so fine. He did not realize he even took the ring. Now he was a public menace and a common robber. Lebron's first instinct was to return it, give an apology to his father, and hope for things to turn out for the best. Yet as he glanced at the surface of the ring, a song sounded in his head, a song of treasure. As Lebron examined the ring, he wondered what he would do with such a beauty. He placed the ring down next to him so he could ponder about the future.

First, he thought, *I could buy new sneakers for my siblings and myself.* Occasionally, Lebron would become envious of his better-off classmates, who gloated of their Nikes and Air Jordan shoes that Lebron could only dream about.

Next, Lebron thought excitedly, *I would buy a car, a nice one, maybe a Bentley, if this ring is worth that much.* Many of his peers already owned their own vehicles; jealousy of those teens because of their cars frequented Lebron's mind. He imagined picking up the twins, bringing them somewhere for their enjoyment while dad was gone. Lebron also envisioned picking up an anxious Sierra, and dropping her off at a Rehabilitation Center.

So many things Lebron could purchase with the ring; he could finally procure the objects he coveted: he didn't even have an Ipod, the impromptu symbol of modern youth. But they all would not matter, for they were too materialistic. Besides, if he would cash in such a ring, he would have to pay back Ajax for two years of increasing debt, plus interest if Ajax was greedy.

Lebron, suddenly enlightened, imagined a perfect way he would hypothetically utilize the money. *I would use it to provide for my family. I could pay off dad's debt, move away from our terrible home and away from Ajax, move into a nice roomy house, and Sierra could move back in with us. We will all be able to enjoy the extravagance of college education, and all our problems would go away. We all would be happy.*

At that moment, Lebron's mind was plunged deep into conflict. The opposing sides would not relent and both were strident. The Medieval battle between two principles took place of in his head. One would sternly command him to select the ethical solution; ethics was a major component of his personality. Ever since he was a little boy, he learned what was right and what was wrong by observing his sister's behavior and conduct. The other side was more casual, and very enticing. It allured him using appeal and attractiveness. Besides, the other side informed, your sister was a big hypocrite, and an even larger fool.

In the end, however, Lebron was compelled to go with his conscience, and made a resolve to return it. However, he was attached to the ring, and could not bear to depart from it. Lebron looked to a pile of litter nearby. He spotted a miniature Wal-mart bag and removed it from the other undesirables. He put the ring inside the bag.

Sierra opened the door again, looking as melancholic as she did when she departed.

"Lebron, I know you are suffering much pain now, but listen to my advice. I am sorry for causing you pain, and I wish that things could be better, but remember that happiness does not come from pure wealth. You should really return the ring to our mother."

Lebron's eyes glared an icy glare, and glistened with the harsh shimmer of evil. "How do you know about it?" Lebron retorted rashly.

"You could see the shine from the ring a mile away."

"I know, right? It is a real beauty isn't it? Probably worth trillions."

"And a soul."

Lebron gave her another eerie glare and asked, "It still doesn't explain how you know about it."

"I saw you extract it from your pocket and examine it. I assumed it was from our mother's car. Am I not correct?"

Lebron's expression suddenly resembled a snake. Sierra recoiled at the face, and flinched when he hissed, "So you stood there and watched me through your window?"

"I didn't have the strength to face you yet, but I'm here now." Sierra replied.

"Do you expect me to return the ring at your command, Sierra? You must be a bigger fool that I anticipated." Lebron jeered.

"I think it's best for you to hand the ring over to me, Lebron."

Lebron's eyes brewed with revulsion and odium. His facial figures suddenly resembled a lion ready to pounce, as well with a reptilian predatoriness and voracity. He gave her an eerier, wordless hiss. Something was different about Lebron, Sierra noted. The ring had corrupted him quickly. It only took a momentary examination, and he was hooked, just like her with her Mary Jane, and her addiction to prescription drugs, except this was worse. Lebron looked as though he would not hesitate to murder Sierra if it came to, but she stood her ground. "I'll say it again; hand over the ring."

"We need this, can't you see? We'll finally have the life we always wanted, and I won't let you throw it all away." For a moment, Lebron's facial expression became sympathetic, but it was merely instantaneous.

"Okay then. I wish you luck. Just remember, Lebron, don't let this ring take over you. It has already started. That is my last warning." She went back inside, but once inside, Lebron saw through the clear doors, she broke into tears.

Lebron, with a newfound devotion to the ring, reached for the black bag he had placed next to him. He had found nothing. Lebron whipped his head around in search of the bag with the ring inside. Finally, Lebron spotted the bag – swinging from the hands of a beggar dressed in rags. The vagrant was running down the block with *Lebron's* ring.

Enraged, Lebron shouted, "You stole my ring!!!!!!" at the top of his lungs. With a newfound profanity, Lebron publicly and loudly swore. With that, Lebron chased after the one thing that gave meaning to his life.

*　　　　*　　　　*

After chasing after the thief for a long while, Lebron wondered how much more of this he could take. There were moments of hope when the thief lost stamina with Lebron still sprinting at high-speed. There were also moments of futility when Lebron lost sight of the thief. Now, Lebron knew, he and the thief had something in common: their legs aching, abdomens throbbing, and their whole composure likely to collapse. Though they still ran, and only pure willpower kept them going.

The thief more often than not tried to use his wit in evading Lebron with no reward. Lebron always caught up to him, no matter what ploy, tactic, gambit, maneuver, or trick he orchestrated. Once, he almost lost Lebron permanently, but Lebron, persistent, mounted on an abandoned bicycle and biked away.

Once they entered the urban part of town, the streets were congested with rushing civilians and relaxed amblers. Despite the crowded atmosphere, Lebron was finally catching up to the thief, when he riskily made an illegal dash across the busy intersection; Lebron was born with a better sense than the wild outlaw, and rationalized that it would be impossible for him to go through without getting harmed. So, like the average common law-abiding pedestrian, he waited until the streetlight permitted him a safe walk across the intersection.

The thief was far ahead of Lebron now, and Lebron had a mind to capitulate to the cries of agony and anguish from his legs. Once he felt that he could not bear to make another step with the excruciating pain he was suffering, he witnessed a person crash into a pole, exit her vehicle and shove the poor beggar into an alley. Lebron made a final dash towards the alley and sat down next to it. He positioned his head to eavesdrop on what was happening. Eavesdropping was something he did well, and he eavesdropped whenever he had the opportunity.

The person who exited the vehicle was actually a young woman, around seventeen. She clutched a gun, holding it sideways for dramatic effect, and aimed it at his head. She demanded the whereabouts of the ring, brandishing the gat for effect. The young thief could see that she was bluffing, and did not take her seriously. Angrily, she called him a coward, and her forefinger lingered around the trigger of the gun until it finally placed itself confidently and dangerously upon the trigger of the gun. The sudden rise in vulgarity in her language and violence in her tone told Lebron that she was not bluffing anymore. He stood up, and prepared himself for whatever would come next.

The animosity between the two reached its climax. Now, it seemed as if the sly thief would not part with the beloved ring. Actually, he was so blunt and plain about it, it seemed as if he never took her seriously at all; this only bred rage that consumed the teenage girl. She gripped her firearm and looked ready to commit homicide. She counted down to three, but at the third second, the thief suddenly threw dust and pebbles in her face. He darted out of the alley, but soon he found himself face first into the ground, courtesy of Lebron.

After tripping the thief, Lebron obtained the ring from him and dashed. The beggar was bewildered, but was able to sprint after him. A dragon provoked, the teenage girl came out of the alley furiously and roared out an insult to the eighteen year old thief. Lebron crossed the intersection; beneficially, the streetlight turned green afterwards, allowing the cars to zoom by hastily, as if they had important affairs to attend to. Sometimes, autos could be so hasty, impulsive, presumptuous, and quick to anger and jump to conclusions.

*   *   *

<u>A Mental Poem</u>

A novelty shop
Devoid
Dilapidated
Depressing -to see how
bad business was for the
owners and employees-

Those were Lebron's observations of an outlet novelty shop he hastily entered in order to evade his pursuers.

He was immediately met with an oddly suspicious yet indifferent expression by one of the two cashiers. Obviously more enthusiastic than her coworker, the other clerk's eyes perked up once she understood him as a customer.

The first employee buried his head in a seemingly intriguing newspaper article, but Lebron suspected that he was truthfully staring blankly at the words while trying to steal some sleep. The second employee greeted me cheerfully and told me of recent bargains, discounts, new items available for sale, classic trinkets, popular favorites, et cetera. She had much zest, and tried to make sure that Lebron, the customer, will leave with a novelty after an enlarged, exponentially recessive time of depression for the humble establishment. After a long time of economic disaster, she hoped that he would give them pleasure by buying a novelty, bestowing a tip for the employees or try to help the owners earn even a slither of revenue.

However, Lebron had other things to take care of than to pay attention to the second employee's futile attempt to gain a customer. Lebron could not say that he truly took notice to even a word she said. The store being laden with failure, it was rude for Lebron to rush into the bathroom for safety, disregarding her existence, yet Lebron had better things to think about than sympathy. The female employee's mouth stopped in mid sentence, disappointed that Lebron was not interested him in any of her desperate offers.

Lebron hid inside the men's room for safety, because the transparent, broad, and enormous windows that allowed pedestrians to observe what was inside posed a treacherous threat. If, by chance, the thieving bugger ambled by, he would be able to see Lebron inside if he lingered inside the store. It was not only a precaution; there were also other causes for hiding there (catching a breath and devious mental scheming), both of which would be defeated if he was caught.

Suddenly, the sounds of doorbells ringing and a door opening rang against Lebron's eardrums. Frightfully, he tensed, and started to tremble as terror filled his head. *There is a big chance that could be someone else. Stop trembling, you paranoid craven.* Lebron commanded himself.

Unfortunately, Lebron's paranoia was justified; one of his pursuers had entered the economically-struggling novelty shop. Lebron tried to silence himself inside the filthy latrine stall, though wincing at the malodorous and rancid smell of waste and other substances. The thief kicked the bathroom door with much power, vigor, and dynamism that Lebron flinched convulsively at the booming sound. As the thief strode through the bathroom, a shudder-quake vibrated down Lebron's spine.

Lebron attempted to suppress his fright, and was successfully doing so, until a stifled breath broke free from the oral chasm of his mouth. The breath was an echo of a dragon's pathetic squeal from the bowels of the abyss. It was not too shrill, but it was loud enough to betray Lebron's location. Suddenly, silence erupted. He stood still, while Lebron stifled his breathing because it proved too boisterous. It was similar to a standoff; both awaited the other's opening move, either provocative or conciliatory, waiting for one to make a gesture of challenge or capitulation.

After a while of stillness, it was the thief that finally broke the quietness. Irritated by his cowardice, he criticized Lebron for his show of cravenness. Angrily, he began to kick stalls open. Lebron readied himself. As he forcibly entered Lebron's stall, Lebron's fist crashed against his abdomen with ultimate force. As the thief cowered in pain, he was struck again in his nasal area.

Lebron made a wild dash towards the window, but the thief recovered faster than expected. He put his hands on Lebron's shoulders and threw him down with much vigor. Before Lebron's brain could comprehend what just occurred, the bugger kicked Lebron hard in his stomach. Lebron's face was petrified with pain as the thief presented him with an inevitable command: give me the ring.

Lebron was still in a state of shock when the bugger grabbed Lebron by the collar and told Lebron of how determined he was in obtaining the ring. Lebron's whole composure became one paroxysm of fear and pain. However, a snake-like anger possessed over Lebron, and he became strengthened by the ice-cold hate he felt, and the dangerous, snakelike maternal instinct of protecting his beloved treasure. His trembling ceased, and his fear was terminated. A voice suggested an idea: *Maybe you will have to murder this bugger, for the sake of the ring*. Lebron did not quiver at the suggestion; in fact, he welcomed it with open arms. *There are no bad ideas,* Lebron replied to the imaginary voice.

Suddenly, Lebron and the thief both noticed the entrance of the outlet store crash open. The bugger's head turned around, and in that moment Lebron made a wild-card decision; he made a grab at the nearby mop and smacked the thief's face with it. Lebron gave one last strike against the thief's face and fled out of the bathroom window.

Lebron ran ecstatically down the street and into an ally. In the alley, Lebron hid behind a garbage dump; feeling secure behind the trash heap, he made another examination of the ring. Its shimmer in the midst of the dark atmosphere was unnaturally radiant. It made Lebron smile. Once he was ready to leave the refuge, he heard footsteps in the alleyway Lebron peeked to see who it was. He found Ajax, panting out of breath; it was obvious he was running from some foe. *I must not let him see the ring,*

Lebron thought anxiously. Lebron remained petrified in place. Ajax noticed him, and gave him a sort of friendly smile.

"Lebron, how have you been?" Ajax greeted.

"Okay, considering how bad times are these days. How have *you* been?" Lebron replied awkwardly.

"I am doing as terrible as before, possibly worse."

Lebron slowly moved the hand holding the ring towards his back pocket.

"Oh well, these things do happen. Am I right?" Lebron said.

"Yes, I suppose so. What were you doing behind the trash can?" Ajax inquired distrustfully.

"Nothing, honestly," Lebron answered ineptly and clumsily. "You know, just hanging out."

Ajax's suspicion was easily perceivable on the expression he wore. His eyes completed an in-depth examination of Lebron; as they scrutinized Lebron thoroughly, they finally saw the attractive shimmer in Lebron's hand that was slowly nearing Lebron's pocket.

"What is it you are holding, Lebron?" Ajax asked suspiciously.

Lebron's heart sank. "I am not holding anything."

Ajax glared at Lebron. "Yes, you are."

Lebron pocketed it swiftly, afterwards showing his empty palms to Ajax in a desperate attempt to end his dangerous curiosity. "You see, I am holding nothing."

Ajax had had enough of Lebron's tomfoolery. "Empty your pockets."

Lebron's snakelike state returned. "Why should I listen to an ignorant thug?"

Ajax's anger flared. With one hand, Ajax pulled up his shirt to reveal a gun tucked inside his pants. "Empty your pockets or I'll blow a cap in here!"

Garcia

5

As she was walking towards the Spider, Garcia tried to look as nonchalant as she could, like a pedestrian taking an innocent stroll. As soon as she was able to see the Spider, she instinctively ducked behind a nearby bush. The Spider was in an empty driveway of a run down house, and in it, the ring. After moments of waiting, Garcia peered over to check if it was still safe. Garcia was about to stand when suddenly the door slammed open.

A late adolescent stormed out of the front entrance of the dwelling. His rage was tangible to the point that gave Garcia chills. Up-close, he looked like he was on the verge of tears. He stomped back and forth angrily until he noticed the Spider. Suddenly, his body started to tremble uncontrollably. His anger turned into a ferocious fury.

He acquired a mallet on the side of the road on top of a sewer vent; with it, he spit his wrath upon the Spider. The sound of shattered glass rang as he attacked the windows. Then, he obtained a partially empty gallon of gasoline, placed it on the car's engine and struck the engine. A barbaric blaze was summoned where the mallet hit the engine.

He cracked the trunk open and remained still as he examined its contents. Something caught his eye, but a screaming lady darted out of the house, racing towards the car. A pang of regret marked the adolescent's face, and, after pocketing something, he made a desperate dash to escape. An older man in his mid forties zoomed out of the house, also shocked. This man bore a staggering similarity to the adolescent, so Garcia assumed that he was the teen's father; the man wore a disappointed look on his face.

"Wow. I didn't know things were this bad." said the lady.

"Me neither." said the father dejectedly.

"The last time I saw Lebron, He was a nice kid, and now you've turned him to a hooligan-"

"I did not turn him into anything. I would never have thought Lebron would do something like this." The father insisted.

"It's your bad parenting. Maybe I should have mothered him. You are not cut out for this sort of thing, I suppose."

"What are you saying?"

"I am saying that I think it's best if I take full custody of my children."

"What? You can't mean to take them away from their own father."

"Well, you've made a big mess of it. I always knew you were a bad father. Look at what you've done to my children."

"Now they're your children. Were you there when James cried his eyes out when he learned of our divorce?"

"Well, I'm here now." She declared.

The woman then proceeded to go inside to get her cell phone. Obviously, she called AAA. Afterwards, the woman ran in the direction of her son. The father merely remained outside, and started to weep vehemently as he sat on the porch. Soon, he just went inside.

Garcia, engrossed by the current episode, suddenly remembered her objective, and went on to creep towards the devastated Spider. She ravaged the car, but no ring of any sort was found. The only part still not set ablaze was the trunk, but the ring was not there either. The thought that the precious jewel melted in the flames was unacceptable. After abandoning the search, Garcia realized that the adolescent pocketed the ring before running away.

Garcia shot out in the direction of the teen, and soon, she caught up enough to see him running in the distance. After a mile of consistent sprinting, Garcia looked for a better alternative. Conveniently, she noticed an idle Jeep on the side of the road. The keys were in the ignition, and the radio was playing classic rock, her favorite genre. To an exhausted Garcia, this appeal was irresistible.

Then, Garcia did something she was not proud of. She did not *steal* or *abduct* the Jeep; those words were too strong, and imply criminal and malicious behavior, and Garcia could never be a criminal. She despised them. She simply slipped into the automobile, craving for some music, and found the keys in the ignition. Then, Garcia innocently took the car for a drive. Besides, the Jeep was filthy, and had countless problems concerning its mechanics. It would have cost more to repair the car than to buy a new car. The owners of the Jeep should be thanking Garcia for taking it off their hands.

She could only drive under thirty miles per hour, and even by twenty it started to malfunction. Garcia, however, continued driving for the sole reason that the soles of her feet ached.

Luckily, Garcia was just in time for her to witness a guy in rags rob the adolescent of the ring she pursued. The adolescent chased the bum, consequently, and shouted, “Give me back my ring!” Garcia resolved to follow them.

The adolescent hounded after the eighteen year old vagrant. The vagrant almost got run over by Garcia, but she utilized all of her limited driving skills to prevent an accidental homicide form occurring. Cleverly, Garcia realized that the vagrant planned to dash towards the highly populated mall around the curb and across the street. As he was darting around the curb, Garcia cut him off by parking between him and the mall, blocking his escape route.

Garcia extracted her handgun in an intimidating manner while making sure no one but the vagrant saw the weapon. Trembling, Garcia wondered if all this was worth the trouble. Her mother was dead; nothing could change that. Besides, had she succumbed into being a common felon, the type of people she despised most? Would she commit such a crime to obtain a ring that she does not know what to do with just to justify the death of her mother? She felt a familiar, faint feeling of stressful misery that she felt during yester night's cutting. The pressure that was lifted temporarily had returned, now more intense than before.

She brandished her handgun and forced the vagrant into an alley, yet she felt that she was also being trapped.

Jack

5

Sprinting as fast as I could, I tried to flee from this teen. Being as devious as possible, I took random and unnecessary turns, running as swiftly as humanly possible; yet despite my most clever attempts, I couldn't deceive him. In fact, he seemed to be catching up to me. After every sharp turn I made, it seemed like he was closer to me. Stamina soon left me, but the same was happening to my foe.

Making a final, ultimate attempt to dupe him, I took a sharp turn around the corner, then crossing the street when I reached the other side of the block. I hid amongst the pedestrian crowd, hoping he wouldn't recognize me among the enormity of walking civilians. I turned around to see the determined dude bumping into someone and tripping. I thought I got away from him for sure, but afterwards I saw him following me once again. *How*? I wondered desperately. I headed into an unnoticeable alley and leaped over the wall. He must have seen me, because the next thing I knew, he was pursuing me again.

Soon, we were running amok in the urban area. Desperate, I darted across the busy street as the streetlight shone green; cars swerved, drivers stomped on their brakes, and people shouted their insults at me. I even had to jump over a vehicle to avoid injury. The driver looked young, and gave me a funny look when I ran past. I looked back to see my pursuer trapped on the other side of the intersection. He must have been more reasonable than me, or less radical, because he wouldn't walk across until the streetlight shone red.

I noticed a Wal-Mart nearby and decided to make one last sprint inside the store. He surely wouldn't have had found me if I hid amongst the multitude of customers in the roomy Wal-Mart store. *I could take the emergency exit and I'll be home-free.* It lay, unfortunately, a few blocks away and I would have had to cross the street again, but I made a run for it anyway. Like a cheetah, I dashed toward my target. My legs turned to rockets that thrusted me across the sidewalk. I didn't dare to look back.

As I was going to make my turn, I saw the car I almost got run over by crash into a pole. The driver departed from the destroyed vehicle, ran up to me and took out a gun. She flaunted me the gun boldly, while making sure no one else saw that she had a gun. Up-close, I could see that she was about seventeen. After shoving me into an alley, she dropped her gun like an idiot. My nerves eased a little and a silent sigh escaped my mouth; she did not know what she was doing. She nervously asked me to give her the ring.

"Are you deaf? Give me the ring!" she whined, pointing her gun at me anxiously.

"What ring?" I retorted. She knew I was lying.

She demanded to see what I was holding. I only barraged her with irrelevant and witty comments that were designed to anger her. I was tired of being pushed around: I would fight back. We engaged in a series of back and forth until she could not take much longer.

"I don't think you know how serious this is to me; I am not playing around!"

Silence.

"I know how to use this thing." she declared, shaking her gun in an oddly trembling manner.

"I found this ring and I wanted to give it to the police," I lied, "but then you came to take it. I-"

"If you did 'find it', you shouldn't have a problem returning it to Me." she said.

I looked away nervously, but then as I looked at the ring one last time, I saw my life flash before my eyes.

I saw pain, misery, and even though I had periods of temporary happiness, melancholy. The thing that struck me hard was that I had no opportunities, no way of achieving anything. I had no way to verify that I wasn't a 'nobody', no way to become a 'somebody' who benefits to the world instead of someone who brings pain. I was a worthless piece of trash; my clone was right. I was born to be nothing in this world. Maybe I wasn't even meant to be born. I was an error.

However, I looked at the ring one more time. This time, I saw my future. I saw opportunity, success, and best of all, hope. There was hope for me; perhaps there was a chance to turn my life around. Anything was possible. As long as I had hope, everything was possible.

At that moment, a barrel of hope poured inside my bleak heart. I had the responsibility to keep hope, cherish it and make sure I never lose it. The ring sparkled in the light. *I have to make sure this ring is never taken away from me. If I lose the ring, I will lose all hope and will rot until I die.* I had to make sure she doesn't take this ring away from me.

"Give me the ring, you junkie. I'm going to give you five seconds to give me the ring." she said," Five, four, three, two-"

“One!” I flung dirt in her face. She recoiled radically and viciously; when she did, I pushed her to the ground. I ran out of the alley as fast as I could. I was about to turn when I was tripped by the very same person who was pursuing me. He took the ring and ran the opposite direction I was going to run. Shocked, I ran after him. Unfortunately, the girl got up and was chasing me, too.

“Come back you destitute!” said the raving adolescent.

He darted across the street, pocketing the diamond. The streetlight shone green and the cars started to zoom past the intersection. At first, I was reluctant to cross the busy street as I did before, but an armed lunatic was chasing me, so I had to take extreme measures. Instead of just running through, I made a sudden yet perfectly synchronized dive on the engine of a vehicle, similar to what actors do in popular cinema. It was painless, but I received some obscene shouts from the driver. Unfortunately, I was baffled on where the guy’s location was; still, I need to get away from the raging girl. As fast as I could, I turned right at the end of the block. After sprinting a while, I was sure that I was safe from the psychotic person. As I walked past a small outlet store, through the window, I saw someone with familiar attire go inside the bathroom. At that moment, I realized that the guy with the ring was in the store, probably catching a breath. I went inside the store, a novelty shop with no customers present.

A jumpy employee started speaking to me, I guess about the store, but I just ran to the bathroom. She sighed loudly and sat on the chair with a thump.

Anyway, I entered the bathroom. I took a few steps when I heard a breath. I knew the kid was in one of those stalls, and he knew that I knew, so I waited a while because I assumed that he would have to either surrender or confront me since I know that he knows that I know. I waited awhile but the kid wouldn't react. He must have been too scared, petrified or dim-witted.

Irritated, I called the guy a coward; if he wanted to settle this ordeal, he would have to settle it right now. I waited a few minutes. Tick, tock went the clock. After a while, I noticed somebody's heavy breaths, saturated with fear and strain. By now, my aggravation peaked, instigating a relentless anger in me, activating a blind fury that triggered me to kick open a stall. No one was there, so I did the same with the second stall. It was empty as well. I braced myself, for I was about to open the last stall.

I booted the third stall, but suddenly to be met by a hurtling ball crashing against my stomach. As I cowered in pain, another fist met my face; blood streamed down my nose as water would a river. I heard the guy escape the stall, but I got up before he could climb out the window. I hurled him towards the ground quickly. I kicked him again for retaliation, and then demanded the ring from him. He moaned loudly in pain, so I told the guy to get up. When he didn't react, I held him up by his shirt collar and told him my newfound truth: that I would do whatever it took to get the ring and that in the long run it would be best for me to have it. He did not react immediately, but I sensed hesitation, fear and uncertainty in his eyes. He was terrified, and I realized that this 16 year old might not be a crook after all. Still, I needed the ring, so I intimidated him a little more until he was on the verge of surrendering the ring to me.

Suddenly, I noticed footsteps nearing the restroom; someone was coming. I turned around instinctively, which was an error on my part. The 16 year old took advantage of the momentary pause and smacked me hard in the face with a mop. He clambered over the wall and hurdled out of the window, leaving me to suffer agonizing pain. That 16 year old might have been frightened, young, and even innocent; nevertheless, he still possessed a motive and a determined to achieve it.

The raving teen girl stormed in the boys' bathroom, teeming with rage. She extracted her weapon again and aimed it at my forehead, demanding the whereabouts of the ring. I replied candidly, telling her that I didn't have the ring. Probably lying on the floor in pain must have compelled her to assume that I was frank. She asked me one more time for reassurance.

Feeling oddly unthreatened by her, which was especially queer considering she was pointing a gun to my face as I laid helplessly on the floor. I stayed silent.

Impatiently, she said that she 'will not hesitate to use this gun' and just because she was a girl doesn't mean she'd hold back. I gave her the same reply as I did previously. Giving me a hateful look, she departed, after looking at her expensive Rolex. As she departed, she gave me her last empty threat; she alleged that if she ever saw me again, she would kill me.

The teen with the ring will not keep it for long, I thought to myself; he was in way over his head. *The smartest thing to do is to follow the girl from now on and swipe it from her the first chance I get.* Furthermore, I felt something I haven't felt in a long time, if not ever: self-confidence. I didn't feel that I could actually achieve something… until now. *The ring is definitely mine*, I thought.

Garcia

6

The bum had not reacted as Garcia had hoped he would. He was obviously shocked at first and willing to listen to her demands, but after the initial intimidation wore off, things started to go downhill for Garcia. She tried to start off with a display of authority by waving the gun menacingly with one hand. But as soon as she clumsily dropped the handgun, the intimidation technique fell flat.

Then, Garcia decided to cut to the chase. “Where is the ring?”

He remained silence silent; that irked and concerned her.

“Are you deaf? Give me the ring!” she asserted.

“What ring?” the bum replied, holding something behind his back.

“What are you holding?”

“Nothing.” He retorted, showing his empty hand for emphasis.

“What are you holding behind your back then?” Garcia continued.

“That is for me to know and for you to never find out.”

“Are you blind as well as deaf? Can’t you see the gun in my hand?”

“I can see perfectly well, but I do not know how it relates to you abusing my right to privacy?”

Finally, she exploded. “I don’t think you know how serious this is to me; I am not playing around!” The vagrant didn’t respond to this at all.

Frustrated she shouted, "I know how to use this thing!", while flaunting her gun.

Garcia's rage curdled. People like him were so pathetic, she told herself. They only cheat, lie, and deceive to get what they want. Selfish criminals like him took part in the murder of her mother. They can't survive on their own, so they swindle their way to the top. Her mother was part of them, and then they murdered her for a fortune. The predatory lives of these destitute bums were unforgivable.

The next few minutes were a conversational stand-off. The bum would say something witty, and Garcia would reply, reminding him that his frustrating behavior would cause her to kill him. He did not take her bluff seriously and continued to play the game he enjoyed so much. Finally, Garcia gave him an ultimatum of a three second time period to hand over the ring. Once Garcia reached three a barrage of sand met her eyes. Her left knee experienced a sharp pang of pain. Temporarily blinded, all Garcia could make out was a figure running out of the alley. All of a sudden, she saw two figures running in opposite directions. Garcia got up and darted out of the alley to see the bum, running for his life. Garcia limped swiftly after him while rubbing her eyes furiously, muttering curses, and tucking her handgun into her pocket.

As they reached the busy intersection, Garcia knew there was no hope in the bum's escape. Suddenly, maybe due to her impaired vision, she saw him literally leap over the mass of zooming automobiles. Angrily, Garcia let out a voracious growl. After waiting a few moments, Garcia was willing to ram though the horde of driving cars. Finally, the movement of the cars slowed because of the red light. Though the bum was out of her sight, Garcia knew that he ran to the end of the block and took a right turn.

Garcia then realized that she did not know where to go next. Then, she noticed a figure dashing into an outlet store in the distance. Garcia jogged to the outlet store, garnering enough strength for her to jog with both legs. A novelty store in the middle of an urban suburbia was an odd feature for Garcia to find. She surveyed the store; there was not another person in sight. Garcia, after noticing the bathrooms, charged into the men's room. Just as she had guessed, the bum was there, lying on the ground. He was wincing, as if he was hurt. This would be almost too easy.

The bum swore that he did not have the ring with him. Though Garcia was skeptical, she knew that no one, not even this lowlife, would take an attempt at trickery as they lie defenseless and injured on the floor. But, for good measure, Garcia aimed her gun at his head, and her finger lingered dauntingly near the trigger.

She professed her intense desire to murder him on the spot, and that he was one wrong move away from being deceased. He did not react radically; he only tried to get up from his pathetic condition to look at her strait in the face. Garcia pressed the gun against his head, and ordered him to empty his pockets. The vagrant was willing to capitulate into her demands. Once she was certain that he did not have the ring with him, she demanded that he tell her the location of it.

He claimed that someone stripped him of it. Garcia, subsequently, asked for a description. She realized that the person he described was the adolescent who devastated the Spider. The bum told her that the Spider slayer climbed out the window just before she arrived. Swiftly, she left out the same window, only leaving another threat for the bum to contemplate.

Once she was out of the window, she could only guesstimate where the adolescent could have gone. She dashed out of the alley and hoped that he went in the direction she chose. Garcia crossed the street and reasoned that because the jeweler was more in-town, he would attempt to head there, but would be caught up in traffic, or he would just go to the mega-store, hide there for a few moments, then head after the jeweler. Garcia decided to ambush him at the jewelry store, and then darted down the street. She was tired of all this running.

Ajax

1

"What is it you are holding, Lebron?" Ajax asked suspiciously. Ajax swore he saw a glisten in Lebron's hand.

"I am not holding anything." Lebron retorted hurriedly.

Ajax looked at Lebron. Lebron had something to hide, something that he did not want Ajax to know. Ajax sighed. Lebron always seemed to be keeping something from him. Ever since Lebron had asked Ajax for an increase in money loans, he had been secretive. Ajax never knew why he was so generous to this kid. *You know,* a voice whispered in his head, *he saved your life. Yes,* Ajax replied bitterly, *he did save my life, but he is becoming an annoyance and a bother.*

After Lebron saved his life, Ajax promised him to repay him in full. "I will give you anything." he recalled saying. Then, Ajax did not know what he was getting into. Later that year was when Lebron had beseeched him to loan the money monthly. Ajax had accepted blindly, without thinking of the consequences. Now, he had to face the repercussion of his decision.

Ajax glared at Lebron. "Yes, you are."

Lebron pocketed it swiftly, afterwards showing his empty palms to Ajax in a desperate attempt to end his dangerous curiosity. “You see, I am holding nothing.”

Ajax felt like sighing again. He did not mean to encounter Lebron at all. He was just hiding from the cops when he saw a figure he recognized behind the dump. It seemed as if Lebron was studying something admirably. Ajax, consumed with curiosity, just came in to have a closer look. He saw Lebron hold something delicately, something shiny. Afterwards, Lebron stood up, only to see Ajax. The anxiety on Lebron’s face was easily readable to Ajax.

Ajax had a lot on his mind. His crew, the Glocks, was losing money fast, and Ajax felt that he was to blame. The other Glock members needed the money that Ajax provided. The Glocks were not a full-fledged crime organization, contrary to the beliefs of many, and Ajax was not a crime lord. They were just a gang.

To Ajax, the Glocks were not an assemblage of ruffians; they were a cohort of outcasts unfairly rejected by society. All they had was each other; the money was just a benefit, a way of sustaining themselves. Ajax’s comrades were all in urgent need of some currency in order to attain financial stability.

He was more than miserable. They were his family. They were with him when he needed a parent or a sibling. Ajax’s motive was to help his financially struggling companions, not to become wealthy. In fact, all the profits went to the six other Glock members; Ajax merely managed the money. His intentions were good, yet Fate thought it was somehow fit to chastise Ajax for his supposedly criminal behavior.

Now Scotty, one of the members he loved most, needed her bail money, and Ajax simply couldn't provide it. Ajax wished he never met Lebron.

Yet, that wasn't the worst of it. Some of the Glock members had become wary of Ajax; they suspect that he has been leeching some money for himself. Yet if they knew he was lending it to some stranger, they would lose all trust in Ajax, and, he fears, kill him.

This would not be the first time the Glocks had done so. There was another female other than Scotty in the Glocks; Mary was her name. She was traumatized as a child, and she had a slight psychological trust disorder. Ajax loved her, but then the Glocks found out that she had been giving information to an authority in hopes that the cop would protect the group. His fellow Glock members had no pity on her, killing her in a public park. Ajax did all he could to stop them, but they would not listen. Then, he started to fear his fellows as much as he loved them. He had a mind to leave, but Jay Wall comforted him. Jay Wall had opposed to her death also, but out of obligation, he kept out of the way. The only person in the Glocks he felt he could truly trust was Jay Wall, but Ajax had not even told Jay his business with Lebron.

Sometimes, Ajax wondered if his comrades felt the same way about each other as Ajax did, as a family. Ajax sometimes wondered that they only saw him as a means to wealth now, but he usually set aside those suspicions as follies. Ajax could not imagine seeing another Glock member, especially Jay Wall, murdering him. Ajax of all people should have no qualms about the Glocks.

Ajax had had enough of Lebron and his tomfoolery. "Empty your pockets."

Lebron's eyes suddenly shone a predatorily greedy glimmer, reflecting a scaly reptilian green, and his facial expression was an eerie rapacity. *Lebron is acting strangely,* Ajax noted. *Was he always this queer?* The sudden transfiguration of Lebron did not faze Ajax, though.

"Why should I listen to an ignorant orphaned thug?" Lebron hissed.

Ajax's anger burst into a dangerous flame. Now, Ajax's curiosity evolved into a duty: he had to know what Lebron was keeping from him. With one hand, Ajax pulled up his shirt to reveal a gun tucked inside his pants. "Empty your pockets or I'll blow a cap in your ass!"

Ajax waited expectantly for Lebron's trembling to start, or any inevitable sign of intimidation- from him, but he remained unchanged. Suddenly, He lunged at Ajax and stabbed him in the stomach. Shocked, Ajax dropped his gun. He felt a little woozy. He grabbed Lebron, but soon a piercing pain shot through his right arm. Blood started fleeing from the wound effortlessly, and as he grabbed his wound with his other hand, some force rammed him to the ground. Ajax's head crashed against something hard… he did not know what. His vision was blurry, but what he did see was Lebron holding a beautiful ring in his hand, with a diamond worth millions. Then, Ajax felt his body being forced up, and then dumped into a foul-smelling dank darkness. Surrounding him were undesired substances, and he felt little critters crawl atop his body. Suddenly, Ajax's vision failed him, as his body was overwhelmed by the odor, the insects, and the waste.

*　　　*　　　*

Ajax awoke to the dank, torrid, and putrid darkness of which he slept. Ajax felt the tiny steps of bugs surround him crawling atop his seemingly dead corpse, yet now Ajax, revived, was as animate as he could be, squirming and writhing in revulsion, fear, pain and the terrible realization of where he lay. The insects, arachnids, and bugs started to scamper wildly all over his body, including his face. He opened the cover of the garbage dump and escaped in panic. Then, Ajax realized the piercing pain in his left arm, and clutched the wound with his right hand. Ajax darted as fast as he could to his shelter, strait to the shower and cleansed himself, yet no matter how vigorous he scrubbed, he still felt the undesirable trash attach to his skin. After spending a little less than an hour in the shower, Ajax clothed himself, and then sat in his room, feeling a little light-headed. It was then that he fully comprehended what had occurred.

The scenes presented themselves clearly now. First, Lebron stabbed him in the chest; Ajax tried to stop him from getting away by grabbing him. Because of that, Lebron gashed his right arm. Then, as Ajax recoiled at the pain, Lebron forced Ajax to the ground. As a result, Ajax blacked out. Lastly, Lebron dumped his body in the trash heap. Ajax looked at the clock. It was about an hour after his encounter with Lebron.

He looked at his wound on his chest. It wasn't a deep cut; Lebron didn't aim to kill, just to maim. For some reason, he really wanted to get away.

Then, Ajax knew what he had to do. Lebron had annoyed him, bankrupted him, shamefaced him, deceived him, betrayed him, and threatened his and the Glocks' existence. In addition to those, Lebron had hidden an expensive ring from him, with a priceless diamond. Besides, Lebron knew too much, and he would surely enlighten the authorities with covert information about the Glocks, landing them all in jail. Ajax imagined Jay Wall, and many other Glock members, on Death Row, afterwards being sentenced to the notorious electric chair. Ajax envisioned Jay Wall's last look at Ajax, and the rough police officer's holding a squirming Scotty and forcefully escorting her to the chair. Ajax imagined Scotty's screams as she was shocked to death.

Damn, Scotty! Ajax almost forgot about her. He had to visit Scotty today. Ajax put on his coat and headed to the jail.

* * *

Scotty was in her own cell, which was a luxury, Ajax admitted. But, the cell was small, as Ajax had seen, and unfavorable for a person who had Scotty's mental challenges could handle. As Ajax arrived during the time they allowed prisoners to speak to guests, his heart broke as he saw the innocent Scotty march into her cubby with her orange uniform on. Scotty looked through the transparent window and put her hand anxiously on it. The look on her face told Ajax that Scotty had not kept to herself well.

Ajax sat down across from her and picked up the phone. It took Scotty a while to realize that she also had to pick up on the other end so the communication could work. Once she did, her voice came through the speaker, so eager and excited that Ajax felt as if he could weep with guilt.

"Hi, Ajax!" She exclaimed gleefully. Her face took on a girlish expression as he she clapped her hands together.

"Hello Scotty. How have you been keeping?"

Scotty then frowned. "People here are so mean to me. The police officers are rough, and the prisoners are even rougher. All of them are just bullies."

"I'm sorry that they are so rough, Scotty. I'll get you out as soon as I can."

"And I do not like staying in one small cell. I like moving around and being free, but I can't. Why don't they want me to be free? It makes me want to punch and kick the walls until they break. And I have tried doing that every day, but it never works. Promise me that I will get out of here!" she pleaded.

"I am doing my best, Scotty." Ajax replied.

"Well, at least it is better than dying. Hey, at one of my court meetings, the judge and lawyers started talking about putting me to the electric chair. I hope they let me sit on it; I bet it is comfy and it will play techno music. I could really enjoy my cell if I get one. That is why it is called the electric chair, right?" her naivety was too much to bear.

Ajax could not tell her that the chair was a torture device so he just nodded nervously.

"In that case, then do not make bail, whatever that means, so I can get my sweet, techno music playing chair."

I am already halfway there, Ajax thought miserably.

"Why do they put me in jail anyway?"

"You are on trial for killing one bank clerk and three police officers." Ajax replied.

"But I was only robbing a bank. They have to understand that I was only 'hustling'. That is what you and the gang taught me: that people like us have to find other ways to survive, that we are excluded from the system."

Ajax's stomach churned. How did he manage to turn such a vulnerable child into a heartless murderer? She was still a child at heart and at mind, yet he led her vulnerable soul down the path of a gangster. Ajax wished he had not gotten involved with crime to begin with. Maybe then would the lives of all he knew and love would be safe? But they were all in too deep to repent now.

"What if I told you that killing was wrong? You wouldn't like it if you were killed, right?"

Scotty smiled and said, "That won't happen to me since you are protecting me. You promised that I would live a happy life with you guys." She sighed. "I remember the days when I wanted to die because I was so lonely, and my parents were *super* mean to me. But then you guys showed up and made me happy. And now they have me in this bad place because you guys taught me how to be happier?"

Ajax stayed silent and depressed. *You are a monster,* he thought to himself. She was merely a child in an adolescent body, but because of Ajax, she was on death row, and she does not even know it.

"I promise that I will get you out before you get that chair, okay?"

Scotty pouted playfully and jested, "Once I finally get something out of this place, you promise to get me out. Thanks a lot!"

They both chuckled over that joke; Ajax's giggles became empty. Then, the guard grabbed Scotty by the shoulder and told her that time was up. She dropped the phone and started kicking and screaming for Ajax.

"*I want to be with my friend!!!!*" were the words she hollered at the top of her lungs. Ajax watched her being dragged away, and then set out to murder the only other person he could partially blame Scotty's current condition on: Lebron.

Ajax reached into his pocket and pulled out a phone and called one of his *associates*. The associate came only a minute later with a nice zebra colored minivan. Though this was not by far the choice of automobile Ajax would prefer being seen in, he needed a ride to the jeweler's store. It took him literally five minutes to get there from the jail. He told his associate to hang around the front of the store and wait for a Lebron to arrive and give him a message. As Ajax expected, the associate inquired what benefits he would receive in exchange for his favor. Ajax wrote down an offer nonchalantly and handed it to the associate. The associate's eyes widened; the associate would do anything for even a pound of coke.

After the associate agreed, Ajax left him at the jewelry store and drove around a curb and parked. Then, Ajax reclined and waited for Lebron to come crawling back to him.

Jack

6

Climbing out of the front door, I noticed a familiar car: a Volkswagen. Inside, a woman drove. She was pale, and oddly familiar. Suddenly, I remembered her so vividly. I suddenly recollected a flashback to a time in the past.

*****

I remembered... being inside a dark place. Liquid all around me, some sort of cord attached to where my bellybutton should be. I was a mere embryo, in my mother's womb. I heard something... arguing: A man and woman shouting at each other.

I heard... sounds... words, and I understood them all. I put my ear on my mother's belly to hear what was going on.

"I can't believe you're pregnant! How long have you been holding this from me?" said the man.

"You weren't around anymore. I didn't want to go after you, so I kept it to myself." said my mother.

"I can't believe you got pregnant!" repeated the father.

"Well, what do you expect me to do? I can't control these things." replied mother.

"Maybe if you weren't such a whore we wouldn't even be in this mess." He retorted.

"How is this situation my fault? I didn't force you to-"

"Well maybe if you-"

"I was only-"

"Don't interrupt me when I'm talking to you!"

"I have every right to."

"Well, what do you expect me to do?"

"You're the father; be the father!"

"I had a future ahead of me, and you want me to throw it all away because we...?"

"Won't you do it for me? I thought you said you loved me."

"Well, that was before..."

"Before what?"

"Before you got pregnant."

"It is just as much your fault as it is mine, if not more."

"Don't you dare lecture me! I can't do this. I'm sorry."

"I never knew you were such a coward!"

Suddenly, everything started to move. I heard a slap sound and suddenly my mom was falling.

"I can't believe I lost everything over someone like you."

"Someone who loves you." said my mother.

Silence.

"Don't you love me? If you really loved me, you wouldn't leave me alone with this baby." said mom.

Silence once again.

Suddenly, I fast-forwarded to right after my birth. I saw an empty apartment. Mom picked me up and grasps me hard, almost as if to stifle the breath out of me.. She told me, "This will be the last time we'll see each other. Bye, bye, baby… forever."

She took me downstairs, and walked outside. She strolled behind the apartment building to a dumpster. She was on the verge of tears.

"Bye, bye, Jack."

She was going to drop me in, when a man arrived to stop her.

"What are you doing? You can't throw away our baby. Are you insane?" he said.

"It's the right thing to do. I can't provide for him, and you're not going to help, so it's best this way."

"Are you crazy? You can't just throw away a newborn baby."

"Just think about it. If I do this, we can be together again, like the good old days. You wouldn't have to worry about a baby, so we could stay together forever."

"Are you delusional? You'll sacrifice your own flesh and blood for-"

"For you."

He looked into my mother's eyes and said firmly, "Don't do this."

She looked at the trash can one more time.

"Hand over the baby." He demanded.

She gave me over to him, and started crying.

"Now, I'm going to take him to the hospital, you hear?"

She nodded.

"You can come to if you like."

She nodded once again.

* * *

I was six years old. My mom was smoking again. She always got crazy when she was smoking. But this time, she was angry. She yelled at a six year old me, calling me a devil and stuff like that. She told me to go to bed. I did. I turned off the lights and went to bed. As I tried to get to sleep, I heard someone sneak in. It was mom. Something shined in her hand. She walked closer to me. She had an emotionless look on her face. I realized that what she was holding was a knife. I sat up. I looked at her.

"Mommy?" I asked.

Mom dropped her knife and started crying. I tried to make her feel better, but she pushed me away. Then, she told me that we had to take a ride in her car.

She drove me around the city. I was falling asleep when she told me to get out of the car. I didn't understand her, but she yelled, so I obeyed. Then, she drove away. I tried to follow her, and cried "Mommy!" as loud as I could, but she ignored me, and drove. I cried, and cried.

* * *

I realized that woman was my mother. She drove a fancy Volkswagen, wore elaborate clothing, and seemed to be painted with make-up. She was wealthy, I realized.

The mere word "Anger" couldn't describe what I felt. The word 'Hatred' was too general for the feeling I felt. This nameless feeling was one I never experienced before. This unnamable emotion was strong enough to compel me to jump on my mother's car.

Everything was a blur from then on. I remember shattering the front window glass with my fists. I especially remember her scream. I remember screaming at her, telling her how much I hated her, how she ruined my life; how I wished she'd rot in hell. She was as frightened as she was bewildered.

"Remember me, mom? Remember Jack!" I screamed. I lost all sense of reason, and sanity as it was. Her eyes opened wide as she realized who I was. When my father rushed into the car, I started to scream at him to. My mother told him that it was me. My father looked at me and said, "Son, if you're mad, be angry at me, not her. It's more my fault than it is hers."

I jumped on him and started to thrash him violently. With every hit, punch, pound, and strike, my mom screamed louder and louder, and my vision got blurrier and blurrier. Suddenly, a flash of light shone.

* * *

I looked around, confused. Then, I realize that I had some sort of daydream, or hallucination. It seemed too vivid to be a mere daydream. It was an eerie experience: the flashback and the daydream. It felt somehow paranormal, and satanic.

I blinked. I look to the street to see a red and black Sedan stop right next to me. The License plate said 1VASS24. It was Lebron's car, the kid who welcomed me so long ago. But when I peered through the whitewashed windows, I only saw Charlie, Lebron's father, the one who kicked me out. He rolled down his window.

"Hey, have you seen a kid, about 5' 10'', wearing a green and yellow Adidas T-shirt, dark blue jeans and black and red Puma sneakers. He has rough, nappy, short black hair, dark brown eyes, and dark cinnamon skin color. He's sixteen."

The person he described was that teen who has the ring currently. Slowly, I realized that the sixteen year old was Lebron! I was ashamed that I did not remember him.

"Hey, you look familiar. Have I seen you before?" Charlie said.

I paused before replying, and a sudden rage rankled inside me. "I'm only the kid you sent away years back. Remember me?" I shouted, suddenly fuming.

"Um, no. Sonny, are you okay?" he asked.

"HA! You tell me. I've only been living of trash and scraps on the street ever since you left me." I retorted.

"Sonny, calm down."

" And I'm not okay. You couldn't spare some shelter for a person in need? Well then, I can't tell you where your son is."

"Do you need a ride? I could drive you home."

"I think YOU need to go to HELL!" I bellowed crazily.

"Well. I'm sorry if I offended you." said Charlie. He rolled up his window and drove away.

"I bet you're sorry. I wish you're sorry. I hope you're sorry for the rest of your life!" I shouted after him.

Lebron

6

Lebron darted out of the alley, shocked, disgusted, and proud of his own actions at the same time. He could not believe that he had not only stood up to Ajax, a person he had reserved a fearful respect for, but possibly murdered him. Though a snakelike voice convinced Lebron that this was the right thing to do, Lebron still felt a warping sense of guilt, dread, and fright. If Ajax was not dead… if he kept the memory of Lebron's mutiny… there was no way Lebron should let that happen.

Maybe Lebron was getting a little too lunatic over the ring. How could anything justify the vicious betrayal that had occurred? And it could have been easily prevented. But no… he had to listen to that wretched voice, and now, he was also running for his life as well as for the ring.

Yet the snake sound comforted him and egged him on. *Ajax cannot hurt you. How can he? You have damaged him to the point of no return. If he is still alive, he would be in a condition that would make it impossible for him to retaliate. Besides, by the time he seeks his vengeance, you and your family will be millionaires. You could easily move to a quiet island in the Pacific. He could never find you there.*

And Ajax knows that if he harms you in anyway, you will squeal to the police about all that you know. He would not dare harm you with that over his head. He loves his puny gang too much to even consider spitting in your direction.

By the time, do not even think about Ajax. Keep your eyes on the prize. You have gotten too far to give up now. The ring is in your very palm! Can you believe that? How can you feel any emotion except pure jubilance and contempt? So discard yourself of your worries because you know that this ring will solve them all. Trust me...

As Lebron was hypnotized by the cold-blooded cadence of the voice's words and the satisfaction of nearing the completion of his goal, he was grabbed by someone and thrown to the ground. During the confusion, he felt his pockets being raided by some stranger. The black bag in his pocket that bore the ring was tugged at and finally usurped by the familiar figure. It was the very vagabond who stole the ring from him in the first place. As the bum tried to dash away, Lebron latched onto his leg ferociously; he would not let this fiasco continue another minute. The bum tripped, and Lebron pounced on him and ravaged him in search of the ring. The vagabond finally surrendered the black bag to Lebron which the ring was inside.

Lebron did not waste a moment. He took off in the direction of the jewelry store, stepping on the bum's stomach. His speed increased as the eerie and inappropriate laughs of the bum rose in volume. Lebron would huff and puff and take a split second rest, afterwards sprinting at the top of his speed. Lebron did not dare to look back to see if the vagrant was chasing after him. All he allowed himself to do was look forward.

Eventually, the jeweler's store was in sight, and Lebron's heart skipped a beat. The great opportunity and magnitude of that building would not be seen by any normal bystander. Only by someone like Lebron in that moment, whose life was revealed to him at that moment. He picked up his pace eagerly and welcomed the voice that had kept him confident.

As Lebron neared the store, he greedily imagined various prices for the ring. *At least $750, 000,* Lebron reasoned.

What! After all you've been through, 750,000 is your minimum? inquired the voice. *That can all be spent on moving to another place, buying and maintaining one nice house, and paying the taxes on the new money. It would only last a year at most. Do you want to be stuck in the same situation in a year? I would say at least $1, 000,000.*

You have a point there, Lebron admitted to his imaginary advocate. *But now that I think about it, $2,000,000 is closer to the quality of caliber this ring retains.*

This exchange continued for a while until they compromised at a $5,000,000 minimum. It took a while to get there, an hour or two, but he finally arrived.

Lebron was close to reaping the rewards of his hard work, to receiving the happiness he pursued through the ring. Maybe now he would have the life he envisioned, the wealth he dreamed of, and the joy of stability. Yet, his life would change dramatically for the worse starting at that very moment, only Lebron could not see it then.

Someone ambushed him in front of the jeweler's store with a pack of goons. Lebron, confused and worried, tried to resist, but failed miserably. They gagged him and forced him into a mysterious van. There, the leader declared that he had a message to deliver, from Ajax and the Glocks. The message deliverer also said that after the message was delivered, he was free to go. Lebron quaked with fear. The noose was loosened around his throat, allowing him to speak and breathe again.

"I was told by Ajax to give you this message. You are Lebron, who saved Ajax's life, am I correct?"

Lebron refused to react.

"Well, for some reason unexplained, you have betrayed Ajax and now he is out to get you. Here is his ultimatum: if you do not give him a sufficient amount of money by 5:00 pm, you will find your precious family in danger. He specified that a *sufficient amount* means the sum of all he has paid to you with a 20% interest, and this is the minimum. He also said that paying him at the bare minimum shows outmost disrespect to him and that if you do so, your family's safety will not be guaranteed. The meeting will be in this very van, in this very place. And he declared that if there are, quote, 'Any tricks whatsoever and the lives of your loved ones are jeopardized', unquote. Pretty powerful threats, don't you think? I can't imagine what you have done to piss off Ajax. Well, it's not my business to know what is going on between you two, and I certainly would not want to jeopardize my payment for my services, but. Out of pure curiosity, how have you instilled this upon yourself?"

Silence.

"You act as if that noose is still around your neck. Well, I do not blame you. As I said, it isn't my business, so good luck to you, and I wish that you will not sink to the level of all those other deceased fools."

Lebron was still silent when they untied him and slid open the van door. Before Lebron could escape, however, the messenger had one more thing to say.

"By the way, if you dare report us to the authorities, you can kiss your family's lives and your own life goodbye." And with that, Lebron was pushed out of the van and walked away with a stiff, forced nonchalance and casualness.

Though Lebron took the threat seriously, Lebron would not easily cough up the money; he still wanted his $5,000,000. He just resolved to kill Ajax himself. Though Lebron's gut, logic, reason, and conscience told him that the resolution was delusional, Lebron found a new master which he could and did find solace in: the ring. The Voice laughed eerily as Lebron succumbed into the darkness.

Garcia

7

Garcia reached the jeweler's store moments before the adolescent did. The familiar 'No Soliciting' sign was up, so Garcia pretended to be part of the horde of pedestrians, taking a few steps back and forth until she finally decided to just sit near the door. After what felt like an eternity of walking, this short respite was enough to calm her nerves.

Garcia always kept a wary eye from inside the outlet store; the large windows allowed her to see who strolled by the jewelry store. Once, she swore she saw the adolescent pass by, but then he was shoved away by a mysterious stranger and disappeared. About five minutes later, however, the adolescent returned, looking a little more crazed and shaken up then how she recalled him. He entered the store and got in line behind the jeweler. Garcia casually ambled towards the end of the line behind the adolescent and tapped him on the shoulder. By the time he turned around, her gun was drawn to his back.

"Hand it over." She whispered.

The adolescent shuffled awkwardly. "Why should I hand over the ring to a scoundrel like you?" He blurted out brazenly.

Garcia chuckled. "I never said what exactly *it* was, but hand the ring over anyway. The gun is loaded. Just test me and I'll prove it to you."

The adolescent stood silent.

"Now are you willing to die on the spot for an insignificant little ring that was mine in the first place? You and that bum never really had it anyway; it was always mine. So are you going to let a case of a mere recovery become a case of murder? Think about it."

The adolescent growled and threatened, but he handed over the minuscule black bag in the end. Smiling, she watched him walk out of line. Content with how well everything worked out, she pocketed the bag and settled back down, waiting for the long line to dwindle.

Finally, victory was hers. She squeezed the bag and felt the glorious shape of the ring inside. Mission Recapture was complete, and there was barely any hassle at all. Garcia herself could not believe how simple this had been. But now, she had to embark on a separate, more complex mission: what to do now.

As she was contemplating over the possibilities, she excitedly peered into the black bag. She gasped sharply: the last thing she expected in that dark bag was a plastic bottle cap pasted to a pebble. The ring was still missing.

Garcia stood up angrily and walked out of the store. She turned around in search of the sneaky adolescent. How could she fall for such a ruse? Before she even had a chance to turn around, Garcia felt someone grab her from behind and place a sharp, shiny blade at her neck. Garcia caught a glimpse of the familiar attire. It was the adolescent.

"So are *YOU* going to let a case of mere recover become a case of murder?" he mimicked with a dangerously insane intensity. The edge started to press against the flesh beneath her chin. Panicked yet intrigued, she handed over the empty black bag. As soon as she did, the adolescent scraped her neck slightly, and one drop of blood dripped down her torso.

But before any real damage was done, he fled with the bag and dashed into the store.

How could the adolescent think that the black bag had the ring? Was she being duped? Then, she realized that not only had she been duped, but also the adolescent. Someone had sabotaged them. Before she could inquire who could do such a thing, Garcia figured it out. Garcia dashed into the direction of the *other* jewelry store. It was in a totally different town, which means that it required more running. Garcia sighed: she vowed to never do cross country.

Jack

7

It was moments like these when a destitute like me felt the pride and confidence of a millionaire. I arrived after miles of running to the *alternate* jewelry store. It was out of town, but it was worth the walk. There was no line whatsoever, a fact which the other jewelry store could not boast. This one was known for its notoriously high buys for high caliber jewelry. But most of all, it was too far away for the other pursuers of the ring to reach by the time they realize that the diminutive black bag was devoid of any precious item of any sort. Only a bottle cap with a pebble attached to the top would be found by the likes of them.

It was times like these when I do not understand why I am called ignorant and unintelligent by society. If I am so dim, how could I outfox two privileged adolescents near my age, one of which was carrying a weapon? I put my hand in my pocket and pulled out the authentic, majestic glamour, the ring. The very sight of it made me quiver in eagerness.

The nature of the hoax was simple. I saw the adolescent and waited for him to arrive. Once he did, I grabbed the bag from him and started to run away. Before the teen could retrieve the ring once again, I put the genuine jewel in my pocket and replaced it with an impromptu replica and placed it in the bag. Once the teen ran off with the fake ring, I simply started to head towards the alternate jewelry store in the opposite direction.

I pushed open the pawning establishment with zeal. I had never heard door chimes so loud and beautiful in my life. The jeweler greeted me with a rudely unenthused indifference. I did not care about the trader's attitude because the offers were what counts. The trader took off her glasses and asked if I needed assistance. I told her I had an object she would want to have.

The apathy vanished from her face and a zealous interest arose. She asked to see the item, and I handed it over confidently. The trader's eyes twinkled, and shone a greedy gleam and she offered the first wager. She wrote it on a small index card. It read 1 and six zeros. I asked whether the marking after the one was a comma or a dot. Her expression told me that my ignorance was showing so I said that it probably did not matter anyway. She took the index card again and replaced the marking with a period. I told her that I accepted her offer. I filled out a form confirming my decision and waiving any prospective lawsuits that could arise in a business of this sort. I signed them all blindly. Then, once all was done, I asked for my check.

"I think it is best if I just pay in cash. " She said slyly. I had no problem with that, so I concurred. She went in her pocket and pulled out a wallet. I started to shuffle with excitement. I did not know the average clerk carried one and six zeroes in his or her wallet. She put her fingers in the wallet and pulled out one single bill. I looked at the bill: it read one dollar. I had seen kids waste that on a single piece of candy. Something must be wrong.

"This is not one and six zeroes." I declared boldly.

"Well, you see that dot there," the trader explained, "It means that whatever amount of zeroes behind it is insignificant. It equals one dollar."

This did not make sense. I looked at the index card again and realized that the marking had been a comma, but the trader, realizing my lack of education, replaced it with a dot. Suddenly, I recalled that the dot was a decimal, and the zeroes behind it had no meaning. If it was a comma, the number would be one million.

Enraged, I shouted, "You charlatan! Give me a fair price for my product or I will be leaving!"

The trader merely smiled. "You signed all the papers. That means the ring was legally my property now. You should have picked up on the decimal trick a while ago. It was the easiest con of my life."

Feeling cheated, I cried, "You cannot do this to me. I need my money, my life, my future, my *everything*…"

As soon as the expression of apathy returned to her face, I tore up the papers and grabbed the ring. As I darted out of the front door, she threatened to call the police. Disregarding her threat, I tried to make my escape. I ran straight into the alley of the jeweler's store, and sat there. The police couldn't arrest me here, I thought foolishly to myself. How could they know it was me? There were no cameras that I could see from the inside of the store, and I doubted that there were any hidden ones.

But to my dismay, two persons in uniform walked into the alley. Panicked and paranoid, I screamed that they would never have the ring, and that I would not capitulate to them without a brawl. I grabbed random pieces of trash and threw them at the police officers. The officers pulled out their batons and pounced on me. I pulled out my unloaded gun and aimed it at their moving bodies. One officer, however, crept up from behind and smacked me with his baton.

I tried to make one last final dash to the exit of the alleyway. But as I dropped my gun, a bullet shot through the middle of my chest. Tears sprang from my eyes and I screamed as loud as I could. I yielded, pleaded, and begged them to have mercy on me. Yet the officers had a mysterious dedication to torturing me as much as possible, and even though I surrendered, the two of them beat me with their bats. In desperation, I kicked at one of their faces and limped towards my unloaded gun.

The loud discharge could have been heard around the world. Yet after the bullet cracked the sky, it seemed like the world, including me, was silenced.

Lebron

7

Lebron set out for that van that he had been kidnapped in. He had to murder Ajax once and for all before cashing in the ring. Lebron had tried to cash in the ring, but he was held up by some random wanderer, the same who mugged the vagrant in the alley, and she stripped him of the ring. Determined to get it back, he found a sharp knife on the edge of the road, one perfect for homicide. Lebron went in the store and lunged at the wanderer, aiming to kill her. Though he missed, she surrendered the ring to him in protection of her life. It was at that moment that he decided to murder Ajax before accessing his monetary resources.

He boldly strolled towards the van on the curb. Lebron's face, as well as his mind and soul, was stone cold and icy with hate. He had some sort of silent and mysterious focus – Lebron did not know on what, but he had a blind concentration on *something*. Lebron now only followed what his new master told him, and so his whole being was immersed in and centered on that *thing*. Whatever it was, Lebron felt like he was nearing it, and the Voice was excited that he was so close to it.

The van was in the exact same place as it was before, and as soon as it was in sight the door opened, revealing the messenger and his leader, Ajax. The Voice whispered to Lebron, *this is it. It is time you proved your devotion to me-I mean the 'ring'- by concealing our covenant with your signature written with the blood of all who oppose you. At this moment, your only opponent is Ajax, but you remember, he may not be the last.*

Your first opponent was your sister, Sierra, and it was at that time I was introduced to you. If she ever acts up like that again I will expect you to do away with that pathetic idiot.

Your second was that vagrant who is only worthy of the title 'trash', the lowest caste of society. I showed you how a little hate, aggression, and malevolence can go a long way…

Your third is the enemy you face now: Ajax. Your fierceness should be applauded, but you failed to do one thing, finish him off! Now he has returned more dangerous than ever. You see what happens when you ignore my counsel?

Your last one was that wanderer. Even though she wore a gun, you vowed to murder her. You lunged at her, and if she did not hand over the bag, her blood would have truly spilled.

Now is the ultimate test of your training. Kill Ajax. Even if he decides to give you money, allow you to keep the ring, give your family a mansion on the Florida Keys, kill him anyway! He has the most dangerous potential of taking the ring by targeting your soft spot, family. The only way to stop him is to harden the soft spot, which would mean allowing a family member to die, but I know it is too early to make you commit to that, Maybe one day though. Now, I want you to kill him, and by killing him, you capitulate your soul to ME. I need you to do this, is that clear?

Yes, Master, Lebron seemed to reply.

In the van, Ajax was reclining leisurely in his seat, and at the arrival of Lebron, he sat up from his comfortable position and glared at Lebron straight in his face. Lebron just stared back. His fingers started to crawl towards the back of his pants, where the knife was neatly tucked under his shirt. The fingers clasped around the handle, ready to unleash the blade when the time was ripe.

It was Ajax who spoke first. "Lebron, it is so nice to see you. Ironic, isn't it, that it was only a week or two ago when we were in hiding and I was lending you money to repay a loan that I thought could never be repaid. But now, you are here secretly giving me money from your own pocket."

Lebron just stared almost blankly at Ajax.

"You have what I need, right?"

Lebron nodded slowly.

He continued. "I have told you before; my Glocks have been suffering in these recessive times. And I do not appreciate the outright ingratitude, betrayal, and deception you have shown us. Now, I want no part of you. I would kill you on the spot if it was not for the fortune you hold."

Lebron felt that the time to kill was now. But he had only one question to ask to his foe before the foe's fall: "What were you planning to do to my family, if I did not cooperate?"

Ajax laughed an evil laugh, and pointed to a contraption he was clutching in his hand. "This is a detonator. If I let go at any moment, your house, with your family inside it, is set ablaze. Any sudden movements at all, and oops! Your house is up in flames." Ajax hooted in enjoyment.

After noticing Lebron's sudden shift in expression from blank hate to familiar terror, Ajax commented sarcastically, "Oh, I see that you have started to sweat. I never knew that the temperature was too hot for you, huh? I actually think it is a little cold in here. Don't you think sixty-two degrees is just right, if not too chilly? Well, who am I to judge what you deem is hot or cold?"

Ajax let out another cruel cackle. "The temperature is not something to tremble over, Lebron. Wipe those tears away before they drop! I will not have my van wet. Why are you fretting so much? I could always adjust the air conditioner. What if, perhaps, you are not worried about the temperature?"

Lebron's fingers slowly unclasped the handle of the knife. The Voice rebuked him violently, telling him to hold his ground and go through with the murder, and that the death of his family would not be that bad. But Lebron realized he had gone too far for an inanimate object, even endangering his own blood. He had lost, but it was better to lose now before he loses a worse loss.

Ajax knew that he was on a roll. "You see, Lebron, I am a very practical and respectable person. But I am always wary. I still cannot believe your betrayal of me. What could have possessed you to attack me and then leave me there for dead? Well, that is beyond me. Hand over the money and all will be forgotten. In fact, I would fail to remember that you even existed."

Lebron anxiously dug his hand into his pocket, worried that the little black bag would not be there. Despite his most sincere worries, the bag was there, and the feeling of the ring inside it was also present.

Lebron shuffled awkwardly towards Ajax. "Though this is not money, this ring is definitely worth at least one million. I hope this erases all my past mistakes."

One of Ajax's cronies took the ring from Lebron and nodded to Ajax.

"Past actions can never be erased, Lebron. You of all people should understand that."

One goon stood in front of the slide open door, blocking Lebron's exit. Then two more stood next to Lebron on both sides, grabbing his arms to keep him from moving.

Confused, Lebron put up little of a fight, and just gave an inquiring look to Ajax. The messenger stood in front of Lebron, holding a gun to his head. Then, Lebron realized what had happened; he had been duped.

"Lebron, you should have finished me off when you had a chance. Probably should have given me one more smack in that alley or stifled me with a trash bag. Don't worry; I will not kill your family. I bet they are clueless about this whole *relationship* between us, am I right? Ah, well, it is none of my business. There is still one thing I do not understand. Why did you assault me instead of explaining yourself? We could have talked things out. But you had to go on the offensive, and for what, a ring?" Ajax shook the little black bag for emphasis.

"You had it all: a family who loves you, a stable household, I bet you never had to hustle a day in your life in order to survive. What do I have? I have a couple of thugs who I have to provide for the only way a person my age can: through crime. All of our lives are in danger because of this ordeal, but despite all that I have done to sacrifice, I bet that none of them would think twice about rubbing me out if they find out about the deal we had. I live in a declining orphanage that is providing less and less for me. And you dare to backstab me with an air that your acts are justified because of what you call 'suffering'.

Well, now you'll have it. As you die, do not weep of the cruelty of it all, or call my name. You reap what you sow, ungrateful bastard." Ajax looked at the gun wielder and nodded.

Lebron wrenched his right hand free at that moment and punched the goon at his left. The messenger shot the first bullet, but the crony at Lebron's right received it instead of Lebron. In the midst of the confusion, Lebron sprinted out of the van. He heard bullets fly behind him, but he couldn't stop. Not now.

"I'm coming home!" Lebron wanted to scream.

If only things were that simple…

Garcia

8

After five minutes of jogging, Garcia had practically exhausted the minimal energy she had left over from the other runs. She ate nothing since late yesterday afternoon. If she had known that she would spend the next day sprinting after a precious yet accursed ring, she would have stocked up on the mash potatoes. But now, she was hungry, exhausted, and sore all over; Garcia was practically on the verge of tears, if not insanity. Garcia could not help but think that the ring was cursed. Her mother died because of it; her father died because of it; those gangsters in the GSGs had to fight off the Mafia because of it. She shuddered to think of what it must have done to its original owner.

But, there was also a chance, a very plausible chance, that the ring could be lucky as well as unlucky. Maybe, the ring could pioneer a redeeming force in Garcia's soul to repay for her mother's decease. The thought of yester night still horrified her, and if she pondered solely on those events, Garcia would gleefully hurl herself in front of an accelerating car. Her body was aching so much that she would not even notice the pangs of death intensifying. But Garcia had a reason to live: her mother's name and legacy needed to be avenged. The only other way to redeem her mother was to murder her murderers – like the ancient words *an eye for an eye and a tooth for a tooth.*

Garcia was too close to attaining her goal to give up now, so she had to endure the pains of the journey like a good, God-fearing voyager … unless she still had that hijacked car parked at that curb…

No. Garcia would not walk all the way back to that curb to drive a stolen car and endanger her own life with her less than mediocre driving skills. But maybe if she hijacked a car that was nearer to her, her first concern would not bother her.

After assessing the pros and cons of the situation, her legs throbbed and quivered to the point of no return; that proved to be the most powerful argument to a fatigued Garcia. Garcia wobbled to the street and held her thumb up. After a few seconds of waiting, Garcia deemed that this procedure was taking too long and resorted to more aggressive means.

Her vision distorted terribly; not only was the vision blurred, but she saw multiple images swirling around each other in an almost hypnotic manner. Despite her impaired vision, she staggered, maintaining an ungainly gait, towards the nearest vehicle, a seemingly white shape glowing blue and red at the top. Garcia wondered about the odd design, but she focused on her mission. She hurled herself in front of the car, and the vehicle braked violently. A person, she believed, walked out of the car.

Garcia strolled clumsily to the car. When she was being cursed by this mysterious person, she noticed that the person wore an outfit almost as odd as the car's design. It was all black, with a shiny, oval like object strapped on the left side of the chest. Garcia shrugged at the sight of the unseemly attire and pulled out her gun and demanded a ride. Garcia noticed that the person's hat was also weird, a wild crossbreed between the casual cap and the uptight helmet, sort of like a police officer's hat…

By the time Garcia realized who she was looking at, and what sort of predicament she was in, Garcia was forced frisked, handcuffed, and forced into the car. She was told to blow into a breath analyzer to check if she was drunk, but she was as sober as a person could be, never once consuming even an ounce of alcohol.

As she fully absorbed the nature of her atmosphere, Garcia wanted to chastise herself for being so foolish: in her stupidity and impatience, Garcia had tried to steal a police officer's car and now she was headed to jail.

Ajax

2

"Should we go after him?" asked one goon.

Ajax shook his head. There was no use in going after him now, or in killing his family. They would just have to wait until they had an opportunity to do away with him later on. It was still of the utmost importance that Lebron was executed before any information leaks. It was bound to happen now more than ever.

Ajax took out the little black bag. If this ring was actually as good as Lebron says it was, maybe Ajax would give him a more peaceful death. Lebron still had a family he wanted to protect, and Ajax respected that. It was this respect and this respect only that kept Ajax dedicated to loaning money to him; though Lebron had saved his life, after a while, that excuse for smuggling money to a stranger became more and more pathetic.

Ajax peeked inside the bag, and pulled out an object of the most unseemly nature: a rock pasted on a bottle cap. In his anger, Ajax let go of the detonator. After realizing what he did, Ajax chuckled bitterly. Screw a peaceful death; Lebron should be tortured as he slowly reaches his demise.

It usually delighted him more when a foe got what was coming to him, but Ajax was too preoccupied with thoughts of the debt his gang owed. Though Ajax had presumed that something like this would happen, Ajax hoped that Lebron had enough class to at least pay him a measly amount. You think someone has your back, and he stabs it instead.

Ajax exited the van on the side facing the street, got on his locomotive and drove away. The Glocks had called a meeting that day to discuss their recent economic downturn. As the leader of the Glocks, you would think that Ajax would have called this meeting. But it was Uncle G and Sinatra who had called it, with Jay's approval. The fact that the three of the most powerful members had brought it upon themselves to call the meeting without Ajax's consent should be troubling. However, Ajax felt the slightest bit of glee. At least his Glock members were operating independently; perhaps one day they could extricate themselves from the criminal world and establish a legitimate career for themselves.

Ajax drove into the familiar part of town where he parked his car, then walked the rest of the way to their secret lair. It was the basement of an apartment building. The owner was being swayed financially to look the other way when it came to the activity occurring down there. Lately, that had been their safest investment when it came to bribery.

Ajax strolled around the back of the building and knocked on the back door. The door guard looked in the eye hole, recognized him, and unloosened the elaborate locks. The door opened to reveal the group in deep discussion, with Jay Wall, Uncle G, and Sinatra leading the debate. As soon as they saw him, their heads whipped around anxiously. An apprehensive expression remained on their faces. It was Ajax who made the first greeting.

"Hey guys. I hope I am not late to the meeting you guys 'arranged'. So, what topics have been discussed already?" Ajax asked as he strolled around the circular table the six of them sat at. They all kept their faces down.

"Oh, this little get-together is just an informal discussion. Not a meeting or anything." replied Sinatra, the only member able to look Ajax in the eye.

Ajax continued to glower over the gang with hips at his side. "Nobody answered my latter question. What issues have been scrutinized so far?"

"Well, we have collectively gathered a basic summary of our spending habits in ratio with our earnings. We decided that our lavish bribes could use a little cutting, and that our extortions are too lax in many cases. Also, the way we pay random subordinates from fellow *organizations* to do errands with our resources is a habit we need to break; it is an extravagance we simply cannot afford anymore and it is also too much to assume that they will keep quiet. And then there are other trivial issues that are not deserving of mention."

Ajax nodded authoritatively and grunted affirmatively to each issue, but he was paying more attention to the expressions of the gang. Some of them looked guilty, including Jay Wall, and some of them just looked down in submission to Ajax or in shame. Uncle G was just angry. Ajax could sense him murmuring heatedly under his breathe. Then, there was Sinatra. He was charismatic, an easy person to take to, and a well spoken orator. Yet he was greedy and stingy, and he would not let anything affect his share. Ajax had not lowered the pays of the members, but he hinted at it several times, and that obviously concerned Sinatra. That was probably why this meeting was held, to stop Ajax before he lowered their shares.

Ajax gave one last look to all of them and smiled reassuringly. “There is nothing to feel guilty for. You wanted to speak your minds and decided not to invite me. There is no shame in that.” Many of the faces eased and loosened.

“That is what this country is all about, isn’t it? Why, I should be giving you guys a gold medal or something.” Some of the guys started to smile and beam,

“Maybe you could make it in this world and give up this risky business. You guys could really set a name for yourselves or at least take up a safer hustle. A more consistent, stable, and reputable source of pay can take you a long way in this world.”

Sinatra’s warm face twitched worriedly at this remark.

“I’m not going to downgrade your pay, but think about it. I worry about you guys. You can’t live and keep this risky trade for long. But what does my opinion matter?” Ajax concluded.

Sinatra replied to Ajax. “Why would we give up this profitable life? We are all screw ups and misfits of society; so why even bother?”

Uncle G stood up angrily and pointed a finger at Ajax. “Yeah, man. What are you trying to pull? Why are you trying to dissuade us from the best thing that ever happened to us? You are just looking out for yourself.”

Ajax was taken aback by this accusation. “Uncle, you know I would not do anything to harm you. I understand that you have a kid you are trying to look out for, and I respect that. But, all I suggested was that you could pave a way for yourself and your family.”

Ajax knew that Uncle was feeling a little down about himself. Uncle had to drop out in freshman year, so he was the most ignorant of the gang. He has a child to feed with a mother that does not respect him either, and he fears that if he does not bring money on the table, his child would undermine his worth as a human being. Uncle's biggest fear was being proved right. To him, he had to confirm his paycheck in as a last resort to prove himself to the world.

"Don't act like you know everything that is going on in my life. Don't even pretend that you care. You are the youngest of us, and you are the one managing the whole operation. I'm thirty, the oldest guy here, and I feel like I'm getting the least amount of respect. But if I was an orphan boy with no money or worth to my name, I would be looking out for my future too."

Ajax was hurt by Uncle's accusation, but before he could reply, Sinatra spoke up.

"There is also one pesky problem worth mentioning…"

"What?" Ajax retorted.

"The numbers just do not add up. We compiled all of our earnings, all our bribes, all of our individual endeavors, anything that the group has spent money on, and we keep coming short. We even searched your documents…"

"Wait, you searched *MY* documents?" Ajax could not believe the massive lack of trust there was in the Glocks.

"We had to, man. I scavenged the document, and everything is accounted for. That means someone had made undocumented withdrawals from our fund. We all spoke for ourselves, but…"

Ajax was all rankled up. "What is it, Sinatra?"

"I'll be the one to give you the facts straight: we think that you siphoned extravagant amounts of money to provide for yourself. It makes sense. Your background, your motives, your pay… you are the only one to record, manage and organize or financial information even though Sinatra is just as qualified. Sinatra said you barely mention your own pay in the documents." Uncle G shouted.

"Are you suggesting, that I take money from the group as I please, to satisfy my own needs?!" Ajax cried out irritably.

"Well, it sure looks so. Besides, you said it, not me. Why else would you start talking like a punk when times got tough? You all of a sudden start telling us to go out into the world and start a career. We started this gang because we knew we had no chance in doing that. I know damn well that you don't care about us that much. Less people in this gang: more money for yourself. " Uncle G argued.

"That does not make sense!" Ajax yelled.

"Well, according to the way our budget is set up, there would be less people to distribute the base profit among, proving Uncle's point." Sinatra commented.

"Besides, you disappear on several occasions. Where do you go all the time? Don't tell us you've been visiting Scotty, because it ain't natural for you to visit that retarded-"

"Watch your mouth!!!!!" Ajax bellowed. His remarks had crossed the line with the first allegation. Ajax could not believe what he was hearing.

"Do you all feel the same way?!" he inquired venomously. They hesitated, but they all gave him signs of the affirmative. Jay gave a slight, almost imperceptible shrug.

"Well, at least I know where my trust lies: with no one!" Ajax stormed out of the room.

Shortly after he stormed out, Jay came after him. "Calm down, Ajax. You know how crude Uncle can be. He is just pointing fingers now."

"I cannot believe all the things he said. All I wanted to do was to look out for you guys. But Uncle insults me to my face and calls me a liar. Not one of you came to defend me, and you even agreed with him."

"Ajax, you need to understand that we are all just looking after ourselves. That is why we joined in the first place. We are all confused about our economic downturn and we are all trying to crack the case. We all want to free Scotty too. But we all are scared for ourselves. You know that fear goes a long way in this business."

"But don't they trust or even care for each other as I do for them?"

Jay paused for a moment, thinking of a response, and then pitched it to his friend. "I cannot answer that question, but we certainly are fond of each other. But you have to admit, it is a little farfetched that you would be looking out for our lives, futures, and goals while putting yourself aside. Your spontaneous speeches about how we can make it in life seems a bit too … ludicrous for us to believe that you would really care about us that much. I told you before: we are all mainly looking out for ourselves in the crime world, and when you, a leader of a criminal organization, start talking about that nonsense, we instinctively know that something is up. I know that you would not do anything selfishly or out of your own greed, but you are a very suspicious figure right now."

Ajax remained silent, pondering Jay's reply, and then asked miserably, "Are there already plans for … my extermination?"

Jay looked into Ajax's eyes and they stared painfully at each other. After a pause that to Ajax lasted an eternity, Jay finally was able to reply. Looking down, he said, "No, there are no plans, but be on the lookout, okay?"

Ajax nodded, and then said he needed to be on his way. When Jay asked where he was going, Jay was only met with a stony silence. Forlornly, Jay returned to the mutinous meeting.

Ajax did not know how he would gain the trust of his comrades again, but he knew that it was their most powerful resource. Other crime affiliated groups were plagued with scandals, division, and turmoil. Ajax wanted to keep his family together, because they were all he has. He has no other friends; in earlier times, Lebron was the closest thing he had to a friend outside the group.

Now, it was a bigger priority that Lebron and everyone that knew about any of their interactions were rubbed out. Ajax would have to do these murders himself. He loaded his AK, put it in the trunk and drove away.

Lebron

8

Lebron sprinted for what to a normal person would seem like a lifetime. But to Lebron, time could not have been faster. Every time Lebron grew fatigued, he recalled the memories of his great father, and his wonderful siblings, and the thoughts alone fuelled him for several more miles.

As he came near his house, the streets became more and more congested. They seemed to be crowded around a scene. Lebron refused to take this observation under consideration. Just a coincidence, Lebron told himself forcefully. Maybe it was just another street fight, road performer, or any other triviality that would not concern his family's welfare and well-being.

Desperately in denial yet irrationally paranoid, Lebron started to shove past the people in the mob. He noticed the scents of devastations, the sounds of wails, and the crowd of people observing. By this time, Lebron was closing his eyes, covering his ears, and restrained his breathing so he would not noticed the thick smell of smoke in the air. Lebron also kept his mouth shut so he would not start weeping spontaneously.

The throng thickened like a swarm of gnats, and the closer Lebron got to his dwelling, the more populated the multitude became. By this time, Lebron was practically plowing people over with all his might, yet he was met with the same resistance as he progressed on.

Finally, Lebron arrived at the sight of his house, but the crowd was now at its densest. Lebron steamrolled and was headstrong with the rest of his energy in a final attempt to get through the horde. Once he got through the ruthless crowd with only a few cuts and bruises, Lebron was about to rejoice at his victory. There was nothing to worry about, he told his deliberately shrouded mind. Nothing happened of the least importance. His self-deceit worked temporarily, but Lebron's deception fell apart when he instinctively opened his eyes with loud wails.

Immediately, his heart stopped. Lebron's legs started quivering, whether at the sight or lack of oxygen. Lebron's mind went faint, but he was too woebegone to be gone with his woe by means of falling unconscious. Many bodily commands went through his brain, like orders to scream, vomit, faint, and die. Yet Lebron's mind went blank and dumb; he could only recognize despair.

Lebron's father was weeping alongside his son. It took a while for Lebron to notice his father's presence, but when he did, Lebron stared at him inquiringly.

"I only stepped out for a few seconds to call the police. I was in the front yard when…" Then his father broke into tears once again.

Lebron looked at the horrid sight once again. "B-b-b-but t-t-t-th-the the twins-"

Charlie gave Lebron a distraught look that told him everything he needed to know.

“They have been whisked away by the ambulance. They are most likely dead.”

Lebron fully comprehended the magnitude of the situation and was ready and even eager to react. Lebron screeched uncontrollably, and with those bellows went his whole composure. Lebron collapsed, started babbling nonsensically to his deceased siblings, spoke to them as if they were still alive, scrambled around spastically, and acted maniacally altogether. Lebron even darted towards the razed destruction he once called his house, screaming “Sasha… James… I’m here for you!!!!!!!!!!!!”

Before he could jump into the dangerous mess of flammable wood, Lebron’s father tackled him, saving him from a gruesome demise. Lebron tried to get his father off of him, but Charlie was too strong. Lebron soon capitulated to his cause and wept some more. Occasionally, Lebron would try to make a mad dash towards the house, but his father always caught him just in time.

Lebron could not deny the truth any longer; the house in which he shared so many loving memories, one that he loved but took for granted, was razed to the ground, along with it, two of the most innocent, angelic creatures Lebron had ever known, the twins, James and Sasha.

Lebron always said he hated the house, their lifestyle, their financial position, but now he realized that he truly had a wonderful life. He had a family who loved him, a great upbringing, and an opportunity to be sheltered from the evils he witnessed and lived since his pursuit of the ring began. He was secure, stable, and had a good prospect of having a future. Lebron had squandered it all on obsessing on his dissatisfactions and ungratefulness.

As that realization dawned on Lebron, he remembered his father, and how Lebron had thought he was a fool for not focusing on the impending catastrophes hitting the family. But now, Lebron realized that Charlie was trying to stay positive and hopeful. His father was no buffoon; Lebron was the blinded one.

Lebron had lived a life of lies, so he lied on the cold ground, waiting for God to smite him down.

Jack

8

The cell was pitch-black by this hour. I looked around the cubic confinement assigned to me. I lay on the top bunk of the bed; the other inhabitant was released the day I was brought in, and there was no one to place in the cell with me, so I had the cell all to myself. The toilet was located at the back left corner of the cell, which was prison's attempt at privacy. I was not depressed at the sight, however; I was in fact ecstatic, for tonight was the night I would break free.

Everything was already settled. The prison guards were either off duty or off taking a snooze after a long, laborious shift. The whole establishment was quiet, probably asleep, for it was an hour past midnight. The cell was especially black since there was not one light switched on in the entire prison. No one could witness my escape.

The escape I planned was not the traditional kind of escape that an average jailor would participate in. I was not breaking out of the common cell, but out of a cage that had restricted me for most of my existence as a human being; that cage was also known to me as life. I was escaping into another realm, knowing that my presence in this one was frowned upon.

In simpler terms, my getaway would free me from this life instead of this cell; I was going to do it with with a rusty belt I kept with me since my apprehension by the police. Though they stripped me of my clothing and gave me a new set of apparel, I still kept my belt with the full intent of using it later. Luckily, they didn't put me on suicide watch.

The operation was simple, and I ran it through my head several times to reassure myself. I would tie the belt to the window bars which were at the highest point of the minute cell. Then, standing on the highest bunk in my bed, I would tie the belt around my neck and leap to my demise. I would not scream, because this was what I should have done a long time ago, and the ecstasy would counteract the pain in transferring into another life.

The clone returned again for one last rendezvous before my death. The clone was beaming, but he kept quiet, which was unusual for the spirit. My twin perhaps refrained from tormenting me because this was what he counseled me to do all along, and like a fool I denied him. Now I see the inescapable truth: there was no place for me in this world.

The twin pointed at his watch, indicating that it was time for me to go through with the endeavor. I placed my hand in my pocket, expecting to find a belt that was not there. Horrified, I scavenged the compartment for the belt, overturning the small amount of furniture that was allotted to me. After scrutinizing the whole enclosure, I was ready to surrender the only chance I had at escaping this world. But my clone edged me on with a demonic slither he called his voice. *Come on! Do not give up like a punk. You know it is in here somewhere. Where else can it be? Are You going to screw up the single greatest chance in your life?*

After a while of more rummaging, I finally unearthed the belt from the recess behind the toilet. Ecstatic by my retrieve, I waltzed from the bathroom to my bed. Unfortunately, I accidentally dropped the belt; it slid effortlessly in between the bars of the confine. My clone was screaming at me by now. *What is wrong with you? GO AFTER THAT BELT AND KEEP IT!!!!!!* Unwilling to let the spirit down, I followed his commands.

I lay down on the floor in front of the bars and extended my elongated arms in between the bars. The verbal abuse coming from my counterpart propelled me to stretch father. Eventually, the belt was re-obtained, and the operation started to continue as planned.

I climbed to the top bunk of my bed and stretched to the window bars that were above and beside it. After tying the strap around the window bars, I fastened the garb around my neck and looked down at the surface below. I saw the abyss below that I would fall to, the evil demons lurking, the lake of burning brimstone, and the place where there were wails and the grinding of teeth. Thoughts swirled around my head. The general gist of them contained this message: if you go through with this, you will have no chances to prove yourself, to accomplish your dream of being worth something, to have the chance to find companions instead of being lonely for the rest of your life, because after this, it was all over.

I started to contemplate all that could happen to me; if I die a shameful death like this, will the afterlife be as, if not more, despondent than this one? My legs started to quiver and tears rolled down my eyes. My clone did not take this reluctance lightly; he floated behind me and started bellowing about my immense stupidity while still trying to convince me to jump. Nonetheless, these thoughts were louder than his most terrifying shrieks.

Finally, the clone decided that he would have to push me off the bed. I saw his apparition lash out at me, and in fear, I took a step back, not realizing that there was no surface behind me. Consequently, I tripped off the bed and started hurling into the abyss. Suddenly, the belt constricted around my neck, terminating my breathing. As I hung from the strap, I panicked, kicking the nearest object and making the most noise. I overturned my bed and the desk, and as they crashed to the floor, a police guard came to my rescue.

After freeing me from the deathtrap I had set up for myself, the policeperson took me away to a different, 'safer' cell where I would receive around the clock surveillance to prevent future situations like this. I did not respond to the officer; I was too busy moping over my recent blunder. I could not even do something as straightforward as suicide without wrecking it. So there I was, too miserable to live and too hopeless to die.

Garcia

9

Garcia was interviewed by various different officers and spent some several weeks in jail. She was in a cell all by herself, so she had a lot of time to languish in hope and spirit. Garcia would tell herself that she was swine. Garcia remembered her past self, who could not even look in the direction of a jailor or a felon. But now, she was arrested for various allegations that she barely bothered to remember.

She longed to have that knife to slit herself even more, to release all the emotional distress she was facing. Now, she gained an odd respect for jailors, who spent years in this wasteland, having their minds rot away day by day. Sometimes, she would bang her head against the cold, hard wall. *Just a hundred more bangs away until you meet Jesus*, she would tell herself, but Garcia would give up and start weeping violently.

Soon, after ages of legal disputes, it was finally decided that Garcia would live in a nunnery orphanage, since she was Catholic.

As soon as she saw the convent, Garcia wondered if she just had been arranged to go to a different prison rather than a nunnery orphanage. Yet there was a large, elaborate sculpting of the Nativity scene at the front entrance, so it was the place. Garcia was not eager about this agreement, but she was glad enough to be in a religious atmosphere.

But she passed the thought aside as folly. But she still prayed on that ride to the convent, and it must have been a magnificent prayer in itself, because, as soon as she entered the establishment, she saw the nun at the front desk. Tears streamed down Garcia's face and she collapsed right there at the sight. For the first moments she was speechless. After the initial silence, Garcia started howling, and in between her bawls and blubbers she bellowed *"It is a miracle!"*

Though the nun did not recognize her, Garcia definitely recognized the nun. Garcia could not believe that her mother, Katrina, was standing right in front of her.

Katrina

3

Katrina awoke, dazed and confused, after a sleep that felt like an eternity. She looked around wondrously, trying to take in her new environment, and trying to figure out what had happened before she fell asleep. It was as if her prior life was a passive dream, a dream that once she woke up, was forgotten, and only incomprehensible snippets remain.

The doctor arrived, telling her that she suffered a temporary amnesic disorder because of a massive injury to the head, probably in coalition with a tremendous shock. Katrina nodded to the doctor, but after the words ***amnesia*** were muttered, she refrained from listening intently. She had other places to put her focus on, like what was her name. The doctor kept calling her by the name 'Cat-*tree*-nah', so it was safe to assume that it was her name. The next problem was remembering its spelling. Did it start with a C or a K? After a while of deep musing, Katrina decided it was useless to waste her memory on this endeavor. Did she have a family? Was she successful? Will she ever remember anything again?

After expressing her concerns to the doctor, the physician decided to tell her that they had searched all their records and the only accessible family member she had was her daughter, who disappeared mysteriously after the incident that put Katrina in a coma. Katrina asked whether she had prior obligations before the incident, and the doctor told her that she was currently a mayor who was simultaneously running a campaign for governor. After Katrina contemplated what life would be like juggling these two responsibilities, the doctor told her that her campaign was suspended and that she would be able to run next term. When Katrina asked whether she could take back her role as mayor, the doc said by the time she recovered completely, her last term would be over. So she ruled out politics from her recovery strategy.

When she asked a description of her daughter, the physician gave a physical synopsis of her: slightly tan, 5'10'', dark hair, dark eyes. Before the doc could continue, Katrina interrupted and asked for a personality and emotional analysis rather than the one being given. The doctor frowned and said that a breakdown of that sort would not be recorded in any official records or documents. Disappointed, Katrina backed off from inquiries involving her daughter.

Then, Katrina asked whether she had a house to live in. The doc informed her that her house was a miniature mansion. The thought of living home alone or with an aid did not appeal to Katrina. Besides, it would be hard to pay the mortgage and all the other bills in her present state. So taking up her former dwelling was off of the list, too.

Then, Katrina asked whether there was a God. The doc said that that information was based on personal beliefs and spirituality, and that as a secular practitioner the physician was not allowed to disclose any influential opinion or information on the subject. Irritated, Katrina said that she wanted a simple Yes or No response, not a tirade about how the question could not be answered.

The doctor did not reply to her remarks and continued with the procedure. Katrina refused to listen to the stiff doctor's drones, and decided in her gut that there was a God, or else she would have died. Slowly, she recalled her past religion, and regained her religious zeal with just a few thoughts. In fact, she was more devout than ever before as she concentrated on her pious piety. In the middle of the monotonous rant, Katrina replied suddenly that there was a God. Exasperated, the doctor remained silent. When Katrina asked what religion she was registered as, he told her. Then, the mind-numbing ennui recommenced.

Over the next several weeks, a group of nuns who made their frequent visits to the hospital passed by Katrina's cubby. When they would happen to come across, Katrina would call for one of them to keep her company. Usually, the same one responded to her plea, while the other's ignored the crazy lady's request. It was nice to have someone company who was not a nurse, a doctor, or anyone who was forced to be with her; this nun came on her own free will.

So, after weeks of confinement to the hospital, Katrina finally voiced her need of some time outside the hospital. The nun thought that the idea was great, so the nunnery set up an understanding with the hospital. For an undefined stint of time, Katrina would live and work at the convent, and eventually when she regained her senses, she could have the choice to leave and try to restart her life. The hospital agreed.

Life at the nunnery literally worked miracles for Katrina, who needed spiritual intervention and human interaction most. Yet the greatest miracle it did for her went unnoticed by Katrina until the amnesia was lifted, which was a long while later.

Katrina was helping at the front desk at the nunnery when a juvenile delinquent arrived to enlist in the orphanage the sisters sponsored ran. Yet as soon as the orphan saw Katrina, she collapsed and went berserk, screaming, crying, bellowing, and praising God at the top of her lungs.

When Katrina rushed over to see if the adolescent was okay, she grabbed her and screamed, “Mamma!” This girl needs serious medical attention or an exorcis, Katrina thought to herself. Katrina started asking for help for that poor soul, and went to call 911. But before she could do so, a fellow nun talked to the orphan.

Later that day, Katrina was told to keep a special acquaintance with the orphan for the rest of her stay. When Katrina asked whether she meant surveillance rather than acquaintance, the nun responsible for the orphanage just smiled and said all will be revealed when the time came.

*　　　　　　*　　　　　　*

The girl’s name was Garcia, and it appeared that she was in no medical or spiritual distress at all. But for whatever reason, the sight of Katrina caused her to breakdown. It also turned out that the girl and Katrina both bonded well, as if it was as natural as the relationship between mother and daughter. Garcia was especially merry about this whole arrangement. Sometimes, when Katrina asked why was she so gleeful, Garcia replied that she thought she had lost someone very dear to her, that she had taken her for granted, and that she felt ashamed for letting that person slip from her fingers without showing her gratitude, or treating her with respect. But now, Garcia exclaimed jovially, the person returned. Katrina was baffled by her explanation, but she usually let it slide. She would occasionally ask who the person was, and Garcia would hush up. Katrina assumed that the person she spoke about was the Lord.

One day, Katrina asked whether she could adopt Garcia as her daughter, and they could start their lives anew.

“I know it’s a large step,” Katrina told Garcia rationally, “but I think we are both ready to take this step. We both are in need of another companion. Besides, we already act like parent and child. Now, I am ready to be your mother, and I know that you are ready to be my daughter."

At this, Garcia smiled, and replied, "You have no idea."

Jack

9

My new confine was even smaller than my previous one. The interior was all white, with cushions on all sides of the compartment. The only structure in the cell was the bed, which was so low and uncomfortable that I would rather sleep on the cushioned floor. The police officers managed not to even provide a toilet; they told me that if I needed to go use the latrines, I would have to use the public one with two personnel to escort and supervise me.

Apparently, there had been several occasions where prisoners with suicidal tendencies drowned themselves merely by holding their breath as they stuck their head in the toilet, or used the sink faucet to beat themselves. Some had even tried to shove the faucet down their throats in hopes of causing such damage there. When I asked why the walls, ceiling and floor were cushioned, they wove me another tale how someone banged their heads and hurled themselves to the ground with such determination that the damage practically cut off all access to the brain. Also, no pillows were allowed to prevent self-suffocation.

The police officers also enlisted me into a new program in which some volunteers come to visit lonely prisoners. Once a week, I would go down to the communications center to speak with the volunteer assigned to me. I remember dreading the first session, hoping that the person would be a no-show for this session and the next ones. Yet, to my dismay, the person arrived to that session fifteen minutes early.

I was forced in the direction of the designated seating area and plopped down on the seat with a reservation sign for Jack on the back of the chair. The mystery volunteer sat across from me. There was a desk in between us, and, even though contrary to the region's traditional security precautions, there was no glass pane separating us two. This was done to allow easier communication. Because of this, police officers flocked the room, trying not to seem visible but very noticeable nonetheless.

The person sitting across from me was a tall, dark eyed, haired and skinned female with pretty features. She looked around 20. She smiled easily, and her face practically glowed with happiness. I wondered why she was so happy, but the idea, instead of making me jovial, made me feel not relatable. How could someone as fulfilled as her give advice to a miserable vagrant like myself?

Yet as she spoke, she had a sort of openness, understanding, and wisdom in her voice, as if she knew what I was going through or went through it herself. The very fact that another human being could relate to me awed me a great deal.

We probed every aspect of my life together to uncover where my excessive unhappiness originated from. Her new positive views on things surprised me. For one thing, I did not know that I still had a chance to pick up my education from where I left off. She told me of multiple organizations who taught how to read, write, and do arithmetic.

After revealing my life's secrets that I never thought I could tell another being, she decided to give her analysis on my problems and where they rooted.

She looked at me, and like a professor, she exclaimed, “Jack, it seems that most of your depression comes from one false mentality: the mentality that you are useless and beneath everyone else. You have the same self worth as everyone else. Many moments in your life you have been hurt and you blame yourself. Because you believe no one loves you, you do not love yourself. You probably do not know much about religion because of your solitary past, but I think it is something that can help empower through hard times. Even if you reject religion, the morals are inspiring. Remember this: you are loved no matter what, and you matter no matter what. You have to just believe in yourself and you can achieve. Your parents maybe did not believe in you, but you have to believe in you, maybe Maxwell hated you to his deathbed, but that was not your fault. Stop blaming yourself for things that are out of your control. Stay positive, powerful, and prayerful.”

Her name was Sierra, and she said that she had gone through a dark period as well. Several years later, even though she felt like she got through the dark period, she was still deeply distressed. However, once news came of her siblings, who had been hospitalized after a freak explosion, were still alive, she decided to reform her frame of mind to the wise person she once had been.

Since that first meeting, I had dedicated my stint in confinement to prayer. Even though I was skeptical about this God stuff, I still devoted my deepest efforts to this new endeavor. Despite my initial doubt, prayer became a familiar thing to me, and soon, I had yearned to get as close to God as I possibly could.

Sierra arranged meetings between me and a priest who would preach about the Lord’s greatness and justice. The minister edged me on in my prayer, and promised me that the Lord has paid attention to my prayers.

Patience, he said, was an important virtue that was crucial to prayer. If one does not wait for God's response, the person could have missed out on many blessings. Also, we all have to be wary of God's will and plan for us, the clergyman informed. Some things the Lord does not want to change for us for our own good and the good of others.

When I asked the priest whether I would ever get out of prison and what to do if I get out, the priest told me not to worry and to leave everything into the Holy Spirit's hands. Willing to listen to anything that inspires me, I kept the priest's message to heart. Besides, the priest informed, he would always be there to teach me math, science, history, English, and theology. Priesthood was always an option, the priest reminded me. There has been a great decline in priests these days, he exclaimed sadly. But the Lord was good, so if God wishes to save the institution of priesthood, the Lord will.

After two months of prayer, I was let free because the charges had little evidence. In fact, the officials said, there had been almost no records concerning me at all during my lifetime. They had set out to fill me in on everything I missed out on.

Yet, out of jail, I sought out that priest most of all. Instead of having a big mansion or other materials that I might have coveted in the past, I rather would pursue the priesthood. It was through faith that a humble vagrant like me would be exalted.

The priest was eager to teach me, and he spent a few years educating me in all that I had missed. Soon, I received all the sacraments like Baptism. Eventually, I enrolled into a theology school with full intent on becoming a priest. Ten years after I had been released from jail, I was already in the process of being ordained.

It was in this way that I, Jack, had found my peace of mind. I wish that many other people who face the same challenges I faced will find a source of empowerment and inspiration, so that they may not end up like I almost had, a suicide victim. But remember, that life is not something to throw away easily, and that at rock bottom, the only direction your life can go is up.

Ajax

3

After a day of hard work in the crime realm, Ajax settled down in his dorm at the orphanage for rest after a stressful day. Ajax could not believe all that had happened in one day: a day of betrayal, sadness, deception, and blood. Yet the day was not over, as Ajax would soon find out.

After laying down only a few moments, his cell-phone blared an obnoxious tune. Ajax awoke, picked up the phone and answered to Scotty's voice. Filled with glee, Scotty told him how the gang pooled in all their own personal money to pay the bail, and how they all called a meeting at the park at ten o'clock pm. Ajax looked at the clock and realized that he had to start to head over there to arrive in time. Even though he yearned for sleep, he happily clothed himself and set out.

At this news, Ajax hoped that the day would end on a good note. If his fellow Glock members had each sacrificed a share of their own personal money to care for a companion, then they must have some sort of connection with each other. Here Ajax was, worried that he was the only person in the gang who saw them as a family, that they were heartless felons. Now, Ajax was confident of his family; today must have just been a tense day for them.

So Ajax drove to the park, when it was dark and devoid of people and approached the place they usually congregated around. It was the place where Mary was hanged, and it still kept a painful grip on Ajax's memory. He had always hated when they met here, but maybe now this place would have a good memory to counteract the bad memory.

At this thought, Ajax became more gleeful; he felt so light that he even had a mind to skip to the meeting grounds. But Ajax still had the sense and dignity not to emasculate himself, so he walked casually to the section of the park where they traditionally assembled. They were all there, waiting for Ajax. Scotty rushed to embrace him, and at her hug, he felt the reassurance that things would go well.

Ajax beamed helplessly to them, and greeted them with such warmth, as if to embrace them each verbally. But, Ajax controlled his urge to hug each of them; there was still business to attend to. The other Glock members, excluding Scotty, did not return the same warmth to Ajax as he did unto them. They kept an icy silence.

"So, on what basis had this meeting been called?" Ajax's jubilance was perceptible.

"Come on, Ajax. Couldn't it be possible that we just called this meeting just to welcome a fellow companion who spent the last several weeks in prison?" Sinatra rebutted.

Ajax smiled and said, "I think you're right, but it's just that this was another meeting called by you guys. I thought I was supposed to be the leader. But, heck, if we live in a democracy, we might as well live as a democracy, am I right?"

The group chuckled forcefully, as if obligated to laugh; Ajax did not like this at all. His positive attitude whittled away.

"I also heard about you guys pooling in to make Scotty's bail. You should have informed me about it! If I knew, I would have given all that I have to the fund. You guys know that I… I could pay you back if you like."

Sinatra spoke up once again. "It won't be necessary, Ajax. If anything, we should be thanking you for inspiring us to… look out for each other."

By now, Ajax knew that something was terribly wrong. "If I insist that I would pay you back, why shouldn't I?" Ajax persisted.

"No need to be offended, commander. It is just that we already have certain *arrangements* concerning our individual pay. You do not have to guilt yourself into reimbursing us; we will be repaid soon enough, Ajax."

When Ajax was about to reply, Scotty spoke up. "Don't worry, Ajax, I already handled it."

At this, Ajax's curiosity flared. "What do you mean, you handled it?"

Scotty answered innocently, as if not detecting the strain in Ajax's voice. "Well, I promised to split all my money and future profits between them. Nothing for you to get all worried about!"

Ajax glared at Sinatra, the rest of the Glocks, then back at Sinatra. "Tell me that she is joking, right?" Ajax said forcefully.

After moments of hesitation, Sinatra replied smoothly, "Scotty tells the truth… but we all gave out of the goodness of our hearts. All I – I mean we – did was tell Scotty that it might be wise for her to pay us back, and afterwards, merely suggested the current agreement. We were merely looking after for ourselves. As Scotty said, it is nothing to get all fussy over!"

Before Ajax could react to Sinatra, Scotty jumped in to add, "I really wanted to get out of that place, and if that means giving up a few coins, I will be happy to do so. None of this actually *matters*. You understand, right?"

Ajax glared at the trickster he had trusted, and nodded. "I understand completely." he said. Ajax took multiple steps towards Sinatra, pointed angrily in his face and hollered, "- That you swindled Scotty out of a fortune, or a *future*, for your own personal gain!" He turned to his fellow Glocks. "How could you let this happen? You know how vulnerable she is… and you are willing to let this treachery slide because you were allotted a small share of that filthy money!"

"ALL of our money is filthy, need I remind you that, Ajax? Also, how dare you accuse me of such a heinous allegation? I merely was seeking out our interests…" replied Sinatra, losing only a fragment of his cool, calm yet intimidating composure.

"I'm okay with it, honestly!" Scotty persisted, but Ajax ignored her.

"You're a piece of scum. The truth is that you would sell us all out for a couple quarters." Ajax continued.

"Well, he certainly has been looking out for us better that you have!!" Uncle G cried, barging his way into this skirmish.

"How could you say that?" Ajax growled fearsomely. "I created this gang, I gave birth to this family, and I helped each of you in your time of need… whatever happened to being a family!"

Uncle groaned. "Not that crap again. We each have our own interests in the gang; that is why we participate in the gang's affairs. Can't you get that through your head? Sinatra cares for these needs. You are an orphan and always will be!"

"So you guys would rather have a leader who would swindle you guys out of every penny you have in an instant than a caring –"

"There you go again. We all have our own hustle; crime is crime, and that is how we survive. The only thing you manage to do well is to hold us back." Uncle interrupted.

"In that case, why don't you guys in state Sinatra as your leader instead of me?"

This time, Jay piped up. "We are closer to that than you think, Ajax. I warned you, but you never listen, they never heed my warning…" The comment was laden with gloom while retaining its sharp threat.

Ajax looked to Jay, who was nearing closer to Ajax with slow, menacing strides. Then, Ajax reeled around to notice them all coming towards him with the same ominous gait. Ajax started to sweat; this was how Mary's execution began.

"What are you doing, guys? Knock it off, will you? Stop messing with me. I'm serious, this is not funny. If this is what you call a joke, you all have terrible taste in comedy." Ajax went on in babbling these sorts of phrases when a sudden shot rang through the air. The discharge came from Sinatra's handgun, yet in it was not Sinatra who held it: it was Jay, the one Ajax trusted, the last person he expected would do such a thing. Jay mouthed an apology, but Ajax was too enraged and injured to pay any attention to the traitor's petty excuses.

Ajax toppled over, but as he tried to get up, the Glock members pounced on his vulnerable body. Gallons of blood oozed out of Ajax's chest, and it soiled the hands of the traitors. They beat him mercilessly, but the person who put the most effort in the beatings was Uncle G. Sinatra merely stood and watched, proud of the result of his relentless deceit and cunning to turn the gang against Ajax. Jay was in the same position he was in when he shot Ajax; Scotty was still confused at what was happening and trying to get them to stop.

“Stop that! That is not nice! Why are you doing that to him? I said *STOP!!!!*” screamed Scotty.

When Scotty rushed into the crowd to save Ajax, Sinatra grabbed her from behind and refused to let her go. Tears ran down her face.

Soon, Ajax felt his body being lifted by multiple hands, and then a rope was tied around his neck. The rope was then knotted around a tree, but before the mass let go of his body, Ajax looked around helplessly.

Sinatra had one last thing to say. “You see where caring got you, what all that nonsense brought upon you? You know that none of us will amount to *anything*!!! We agreed on that during the formation of the Glocks. Yet, you still insist on calling us your brothers when you know we are all in this only for the cash. WE look out only for ourselves because no one else gives a damn! That is the true art of hustling, to only look out for your own needs. Any true gangster knows that they should never let emotions and business intertwine. The only way to survive is to be heartless. You’ve been a weakling of a leader. All you can say to reassure us is that we have each other. Do you think we care! Do you think *I* care? Can you cash in togetherness? The worst part of it all is that we all know that you don’t care about us either, especially me… you have always hated me. The only person you even have an inkling of care for is that mental idiot Scotty and you were still willing to watch her get jailed up as you kept stealing our money. You were hustling all along. No normal person, let alone orphan, can tell us all the crap you have told us with a straight face unless that person is a liar. You can siphon millions of dollars from us as long as we foolishly think that you actually care. But you don’t, no one does. Now, you’ve got what’s coming to you!”

Ajax noticed that Sinatra lost his cool, indifferent composure. A few moments later, after blurting out his speech, Sinatra settled himself down and his signature poise attitude resumed.

Ajax could not believe that after all this time they still could not believe that he truly loved them. Ajax would call them all morons, but he knew that he himself was the stupid one. Mary had cared for this group of heartless thugs; Ajax had similarly kept a place in his heart for the Glocks. Yet, look where that got them; the same result: death by their hands.

He knew, all along, that he only used them as a substitution for the family he always wanted to have, but never had. He always wanted a brother, a sister, a father, a mother… he thought he had that.

Ajax looked around one last time. He was met with mostly uncaring, and even bloodthirsty, eyes and stares. Not one of them felt at least a little sorry for him. Only Scotty shed a tear for him. Even though Jay had gained Ajax's trust and deepest friendship, he watched silently as he watched the death of Mary. Ajax saw the cruelty in all of this, in the crime business. What point was there in all those murders, extortions, ultimatums, robberies, bribes, and other unspeakable felonies? It served absolutely no purpose at all; in fact, it made Ajax's last moments even more suffering.

Ajax realized that Scotty also worried over them, even more blindly than he himself. He wanted to shout a warning, to get away from these people as soon as possible, but not to go back to her abusive home, but run away and find a place for herself in the world. He didn't want to let her make the same mistake he did. But Ajax was tottering on the fence between consciousness and unconsciousness, and the mere thought of being choked stifled his breathe.

Finally, Ajax felt the hands leave from under him. Ajax did not know what hurt more, those final regrets, their treacherous eyes, or death itself.

Lebron

9

The car ride to the hospital was the most suspenseful ten minutes of Lebron's life. He knew that the twins were dead, yet there was still a great disbelief that something so common and precious to him would be yanked away that cruelly. At the hospital, the nurse at the front desk asked them to wait in the lobby until further notice. In the dreaded room, Charlie and Lebron met with Sierra, who had also been informed. They hugged, and then sat down in solemn silence. They waited, and waited, and waited some more. Something about the waiting room at any healthcare establishment brings an almost inhumane apprehension. The suspense was amplified for the family. The tension was too much for Lebron. He was restless, shuffling his feet, biting off his nails, and tousled his hair. Finally, the nurse called the name of Vassaux, and the three of them stood up, clutching each other's hands, and tiptoed towards the door leading to the patient's quarters.

They sat in an empty room designated for Sasha and James Vassaux, and the anticipation nearly consumed their souls. In this way, they found themselves in a similar situation they found themselves in earlier: the dreadful awaiting. Lebron's eyes had watered up, as if the tears were at the ready for launch. The three of their souls rankled unceasingly, until finally, the doctor strode in, like a savior.

The doctor's expression gave no hint to what he would say next. He greeted us, and asked us if we were comfortable. Irritated at the trivialities, Charlie inquired if his two children were alive. The doctor took a deep breath and looked Charlie straight in the eye and told him that his children were alive.

Charlie started weeping tears of joy and thanked the doctor. Sierra joined her father in his joyful weeping. Lebron fell from his seat and bent over in servile genuflection to God. Obviously, this sort of reaction was the one the doctor was trying to avoid. The doctor tried to make the commotion subside, but they continued to celebrate.

In hopes of getting those wild ruffians under control, the doctor started telling the bad news. The twins had high degree burns, and would have to receive intensive medical care at the emergency center for approximately three plus months. That did not even dampen their fervor by just a tad. Charlie merely asked, "Will they be okay after that?" The doctor told him yes, and with that, the celebrating recommenced.

*   *   *

By the time Sasha and James returned home, everything had been arranged and settled. The family rented a half of a duplex in a different city. Sierra left her apartment and decided to live with the family once more.

All the legal drama between Susan and Charlie eventually escalated into a lawsuit, but the family oddly did not worry at all over this impending danger. They let the lawsuit be, and placed their faith in each other. After months of judicial dispute, the case was dropped.

The financial strains the family never truly ended, but because the family didn't focus on this lingering issue, it did not bother them at all. In fact, Lebron did not know why he was all worked up over this before; to this day, he could not understand why he got himself and his family into so much trouble over such nonsense.

His relationship with his family members, including Sierra and his father Charlie, strengthened, and the admiration he had of them blossomed.

In this way, Lebron's family achieved the happiness and stability they had been looking for. They had it in themselves all along.

ABOUT THE AUTHOR

Arslay Joseph was born on April 1st, 1998 in Miami, Florida. He was born to two Haitian parents, Ancelet and Casimir Joseph. He has three younger brothers: Benedict, Hantz, and Ray. Hantz is currently suffering from Autism, and because of this, his family of six moved up to Massachusetts to find more opportunities for him in 2009. Always being an avid reader, Arslay began writing in middle school and, with the help of loving family and friends, finished writing this book when he was just 12 years old.

Made in the USA
Middletown, DE
28 July 2015